MW01593648

Uncle Sam's Boys as Lieutenants

by H. Irving Hancock

CHAPTER I

THE LETTER FROM THE WAR DEPARTMENT

"WHEW, but it's hot here!" grumbled Sergeant Noll Terry, of the United States Army.

"That's an odd complaint to hear from a young man who served so actively for two years in the tropics," laughed Mrs. Overton, a short, plump, middle-aged matron.

"Well, Mother, it is a hot day," put in Sergeant Hal Overton quietly.

"Yes, it is," agreed Hal's mother, "though you two, who came from the Philippines the very picture of health can't feel the weather to-day much. New Jersey isn't in the tropics."

Hal's mother said that with an air of finality. Her son and his chum had been through the most strenuous forms of active army service in Uncle Sam's colonial possessions, the Philippine Islands. If they could endure the heat in that tropical belt, even that day's broiling weather at home must seem cool by comparison.

"I suppose you have an idea, Mother, that the nearer you go to the equator the hotter the weather gets."

"Well, isn't it so?" challenged Mrs. Overton.

"It may be, as far as actual degrees of heat are marked off on the thermometer," explained Sergeant Hal. "But I'll stick to it, Mother, that the average of weather that we struck in the Philippines was not nearly so disagreeable as the weather is here to-day."

"That's so," nodded youthful Sergeant Terry, with emphasis.

"I don't understand that," replied Mrs. Overton, looking a good deal puzzled.

"I don't pretend to understand it, either, Mother," Hal continued. "But it's a fact that there are very few spots in the actual tropics that seem so disagreeable as are New York City and some places in New Jersey in the heated terms of July and August."

"That astonishes me," declared Mrs. Overton. "I have always supposed that, the further south one goes in summer, the hotter one finds it. So New York City is hotter in summer than the tropics?"

"It seems hotter," Sergeant Hal affirmed.

The boys were more or less inclined to joke Mrs. Overton, because, while there are many pleasant days in the tropics, particularly near the coast, the weather is for the most part undeniably hot and oppressive.

"Anyhow," remarked Noll, philosophically, "the hardest thing we have to do here is to walk a short distance down the street and buy another ice cream."

"I'd rather be working," retorted Hal quickly. "I'd rather be doing anything than lying idly around like this!"

"Henry!" cried his mother reproachfully. She was sure to be hurt or angry when she addressed him so formally. "Don't you care anything about being at home, after you've been away from us for more than three years?"

3

"Of course I care about being home, Mother," Sergeant Hal made haste to rejoin, as he rose, went over and kissed her. "But I don't believe you can gain a hundredth of an idea as to the suspense Noll and I are under at present. When we get our orders from the War Department we'll know—one way or the other."

"Oh, you're safe enough for your commission as second lieutenant, Hal," Noll broke in. "I only wish I felt half as safe for myself as I do for you."

"It doesn't seem fair that you shouldn't both get your commissions as second lieutenants," murmured Mrs. Overton. "You're both certain that you passed your final examinations at Fort Leavenworth."

"We'd both get our commissions, Mother, if there were vacancies enough. However, this year fifty-nine young soldiers passed their final examinations, and there are only forty-two vacancies to be filled from the ranks. Consequently, seventeen of us——"

"It isn't fair," broke in Mrs. Overton, with all a mother's logic where her son is concerned. "All of you who passed ought to be appointed officers in the Army."

"Seventeen of us won't be," sighed Hal.

Ever since their first enlistment Hal and Noll had been imbued with the ambition to rise from the ranks, and become officers. This promotion from the ranks is not as simple a matter as young people might gain from reading the stories of some misinformed authors who know nothing of actual military service. The enlisted man who would rise from the ranks must first of all be sure that his military record is fine and clean, and that his reputation for coolness and bravery is firmly established. But this is only the beginning for the ambitious soldier in the ranks. He must study almost incessantly, for, when his turn comes to be promoted to a second lieutenancy, he must be fitted to take a stiff academic examination and pass it with credit. That examination, in Sergeant Noll's grim description, "is enough to make a college professor's hair turn gray." There is no easy way of rising from the ranks to become an officer.

Hal and Noll, following the method provided by law, had gone up for their preliminary examinations in the Philippines. Both had succeeded in passing, though Noll was much nearer the bottom of the list than his chum. Then, a good many months later, both young sergeants had been ordered home from the Philippines, that they might undergo their final examination for commissions. As they were "up" for commissions in the infantry arm of the service, these two youthful soldiers were sent before a board of Army officers at Fort Leavenworth. In the interval between the examinations both young soldiers had studied harder than ever. They believed that they had passed these final examinations in July. They had then been ordered to their homes to await the action of the War Department. It was now well along in August.

"You haven't either one of you appeared on the street in your Army uniforms since you returned home," remarked Mrs. Overton, presently. "Noll, why don't you put on your uniform to-night and bring your mother over here? Then Hal can put on his uniform and you can both take your mothers out this evening. Don't you suppose that, when American women give their sons up to the Army, these same women like once in a while to be seen in public with their sons in uniform?"

4

"Why, yes, we can do that, of course, Mrs. Overton," Noll agreed readily. "But wouldn't you rather wait a few days and see if we don't obtain the right to wear *officers'* uniforms?"

"That won't happen in ages," declared Hal's mother warmly. "Every one over in Washington is sound asleep during these hot days. Mrs. Terry and I will have to wait until winter if we must wait to see you both put on lieutenants' uniforms."

"I'm horribly afraid that my mother will have to wait even longer than that," sighed Noll.

Tr-r-r-r-rill! sounded a shrill whistle up the street.

"I wonder if he's coming here?" murmured Mrs. Overton nervously.

Tr-r-r-rill! "Overton!" sounded the postman's voice. "Oh—young Overton!"

Hal fairly bounded out of the little parlor, through the short hallway, and pulled the front door open.

"Good afternoon, Mr. Colton," was Hal's almost shaky greeting. Hal had known this postman ever since the young soldier had been a boy in his first trousers.

"Good afternoon, Hal," rejoined the postman. "One letter—for you. I'll be back to ask you about it to-morrow morning."

Hal stood in the doorway, almost dazed. It was a long, official-looking envelope that he held in his hand. Up in one corner he made out the words, "War Department—Official Business."

Then, still clutching the envelope, Hal walked unsteadily back into the little parlor.

"By George—he's *got* it!" almost shouted Noll. "What's—what's the real word, Hal?"

Noll was now standing on his feet, actually trembling.

Mrs. Overton fairly flew to her son.

"What is it, Hal? What's the answer?" she demanded, in a shaking voice that was but little above a whisper.

"It's—it's addressed, 'Lieutenant Henry Overton, U. S. A.,'" replied Hal, turning the envelope so that his mother might read. But a sudden rush of mist to her eyes made the letters blur.

"Whoop!" let out Sergeant Noll. "Hal, you've won out!"

"Why don't you open the envelope?" asked Mrs. Overton tremulously.

"I'm afraid I'm almost too dizzy to think of anything," answered Hal in a strained voice.

For answer his eager mother snatched the envelope from his hands, caught up her sewing scissors from a table, and held the envelope up to the light.

"Now, take out your letter, Hal, as quickly as you can, and let us know what it says," commanded Mrs. Overton.

Hal withdrew the letter from the envelope. It was from the adjutant general of the Army, stating that Hal had passed the examinations and that the President had just appointed him, *ad interim*, a second lieutenant of infantry in the United States Army.

5

"Now, what's the meaning of that awful '*ad interim*'?" demanded Mrs. Overton.

"Why, you see, Mother, Congress isn't in session just now——"

"I don't see what that has to do with——"

"Why, Mother, officers are appointed by the President, and——"

"And it's none of Congress's business!"

"All appointments to commissions in the Army and Navy, Mother, are made by the President, subject to the approval of the Senate——"

"I just knew there was some string to it all," cried Mrs. Overton.

"As a matter of form the Senate has to approve. But the Senate rarely ever refuses to confirm the President's full list of appointments for the Army and Navy."

"Tell me this, Hal: Is there a bootblack at the Capitol in Washington?"

"I—I think it very likely that there is at least one, Mother."

"Then we'll find out that the bootblack has to be consulted, too, my boy, before we're at all sure that you're really an Army officer."

"Oh, no, Mother," laughed Hal. "I feel just as sure, at this moment, that I'm a second lieutenant in the Army as I shall ever feel."

"I—I hope so," sighed his mother. "But I—well, I'm afraid I don't trust any one in Washington any too thoroughly."

Hal laughed heartily. He had got over the first electric shock of the news, and was happy enough now to laugh at anything.

"Noll, I hope you——" began Mrs. Overton, overflowing with generosity. "Why—where is—what has become of that boy? He was here a moment ago!"

It was certain enough now that Noll Terry was nowhere about.

"Mother," said Hal wisely, "you needn't look for Noll. He's beating a nine-second sprint to his own house."

"He didn't need——"

"Don't you understand? Noll is traveling hot-foot to his own roof to see if the postman on that route has left a long envelope for *him*."

"Poor boy! I hope he has won his commission, too," sighed Mrs. Overton, wistfully.

"Oh, I think he has."

"He's a nice boy."

"Mother, he's one of the very best fellows in the world."

"I suppose Mr. Ad Interim will have a lot to say about Noll's commission, too," said Hal's mother.

"*Ad interim* is Latin, Mother. It means 'in the time between,' or something like that."

"Oh," smiled Mrs. Overton. "I didn't know but Ad was the bootblack at the Capitol."

"I feel like running right after Noll," murmured Hal.

"Don't you dare do it, my son. Don't you feel that I've any right to my boy's company in the first moments that such good news has come to him? Hal, I'm thinking how you'll look in your new uniforms—*ad interim*. Will you order a uniform at once?"

"No; I rather think I won't."

"Why!" demanded Mrs. Overton, eagerly.

"Mother, you may think me reckless, and over-confident. But the fact is, I've already been measured for my new uniforms."

"When? And when will they be here?"

"Do you remember the big mahogany chest that I brought with me from the Philippines, Mother?"

"Yes."

"Well, the whole outfit of uniforms is packed in that chest."

"Henry Overton—you take me right upstairs and unlock that chest—this instant!"

"Come on, Mother!" Hal called back, gayly, as he darted out of the parlor and up the front stairs.

"And they've been here all this time," panted the mother, as her officer-son brought out his key-ring and fumbled at the lock of the mahogany chest. "And you—you—you told me the chest held clothes of yours."

"Well, that wasn't a lie was it, Mother?" Hal threw up the lid and lifted out a tray. "Now, wade into 'em. Look 'em over to your heart's content. Here's the dress sword. Isn't it a beauty?"

Gripping the scabbard with his left hand, Hal drew out the handsome blade with a flourish.

"Ugh! I don't like it, except to look at," shuddered his mother. "I hope my son will never have any need to cut up a fellow-being with that sword."

"Hardly likely," chuckled Hal. "An officer carries only a cane or a stick of some sort just in order that he may point out the location of the enemy, or to indicate some tree on the other side that he thinks has a sharp-shooter up among the foliage, and, of course, he wears his heavy service revolver."

"And an officer never leads a charge, flourishing his sword?"

"Hardly. The officer would be in too much danger from the bullets of his own men if he got in front of them."

"Then an officer isn't in so very much danger, after all," guessed Mrs. Overton, speaking in a tone of relief. "Some one in front of him will stop the bullets."

"No one man can stop a bullet that's going under full steam, Mother. At two or three hundred yards' range, to-day, a bullet will pass through six or eight men in succession, if there are that many men in its path."

"I—I guess I don't want to hear any more of that kind of stuff," shivered the little woman. "It all sounds—awfully dangerous!"

But Hal's mother was not idle. With the deft fingers of a woman she was lifting and laying out the handsome uniforms one by one.

"Here's the one I want you to wear when you go out with your father and me this evening," she said, holding up the full-dress uniform.

Hal laid down the sword he had been examining, stepped over and placed an arm around his mother's waist.

"Mother, dear, I'm afraid you don't understand. An officer, when away from troops and duty, rarely wears his uniform in public. It would be looked upon as a foolish piece of vanity on his part."

"But you wore your sergeant's uniform when you first came home."

"All I can say, Mother, is that the two cases are different. One of these days you'll understand just why an enlisted man goes off post in uniform, and an officer, when away from his duties, ordinarily wears citizen's dress. But here's one uniform, Mother, that I can wear at home in hot weather."

He lifted two garments from near the bottom of the box.

"Why, that's only a set of tennis flannels," objected his mother.

"It's part of an officer's prescribed uniform, just the same," Hal assured her.

"But there's no gold lace, no braid, no shoulder-straps—nothing." Mrs. Overton's voice quivered with disappointment.

"Here's the red sash that goes with the trousers," smiled Hal, bringing to light the article he had named. "That gives the suit quite a gay and military appearance, as you'll soon see."

"It doesn't look like much more than any clerk might wear," remarked Mrs. Overton, doubtfully.

"It isn't meant to. This flannel undress is intended for an officer to wear when he doesn't want to look conspicuous among civilians. I'll go to my room and put it on presently, and then I think you'll like it a whole lot better."

"Maybe," said Mrs. Overton doubtfully.

"All this time," pursued Lieutenant Hal, "I'm wondering whether Noll had found a letter waiting for him at his home, and whether his news was as fine as mine."

"You up there, Hal?" called a voice from below—Noll's.

"Charge!" yelled back the young lieutenant.

Up the stairs very sedately came Noll Terry. His appearance proclaimed the story. He was wearing the tennis flannel undress, red sash and all.

CHAPTER II

BUNNY HEPBURN UP TO OLD TRICKS

"CONGRATULATIONS, old chum!" cried Hal Overton, striding across the room and holding out his hand.

The two friends joined hands in a fervent clasp.

"Yes; I got my letter, and the news was satisfactory," said Noll, in a queer, half-choking voice.

"A letter from Mr. Ad Interim?" asked Mrs. Overton, making a little face.

"Why, that's the only sort of an appointment that a fellow can get in summer, when there's no Senate in session, Mrs. Overton," Noll replied. "But it's all right. The Senate never heard of either of us, and so the Senators won't have anything against us. We'll get our commissions, all right, soon after the next Congress convenes. Our commissions are safe enough."

"Quite," agreed Hal. "That's what I've been trying to tell Mother."

"A new second lieutenant is only a shave-tail, at best," smiled Noll.

"What does that mean?" demanded Mrs. Overton quickly.

"I don't know," Noll replied. "It's just an Army term of derision for a very new young officer, I guess."

"And a second lieutenant soon becomes a 'goat,'" Hal added.

"That isn't a nice word," retorted Mrs. Overton. "It's slang!"

"It's worse than slang in the Army," laughed Hal. "The army 'goat' is the very new officer who has a lot of extra duties thrust upon him that the older officers don't want. Those duties of the 'goat' are generally both very trifling and very annoying."

"Then it isn't right," declared Hal's mother, with an air of conviction. "No one ought to annoy a young man who has been smart enough to make an officer of himself. What are a second lieutenant's duties?"

"Well," replied Noll quizzically, "for one thing he must see that every one of his colonel's eight pairs of boots are kept polished."

"Oliver Terry!" remonstrated Mrs. Overton.

"And see to it that the grass is kept mowed on the colonel's lawn," added Hal.

"A new second lieutenant is expected to relieve the colonel's wife's nurse-girl in taking care of headquarters' kids on Wednesday and Saturday afternoons——" continued Noll.

"Also groom the colonel's horses," added Hal.

"I don't believe a word of that," declared Mrs. Overton, whereat both very new young officers laughed heartily.

"And you're starting in badly, too," continued Hal's mother accusingly. "I happen to know this much—that an officer must have too much honor to stoop to telling lies. And that he's court-martialed and driven out of the service if he does. So be careful."

Hal soon excused himself, going to his own room, leaving Noll to entertain his mother. When Lieutenant Overton came back he was in his flannel undress, red sash and all.

"That doesn't look so very bad, after all," declared Mrs. Overton, viewing her erect, stalwart young son with an approval which she made no effort to hide.

Then they talked on until at last Lieutenant Noll glanced at his watch.

"I must be going," he said, rising. "I've overstayed my leave. Mother allowed me to leave her only long enough to run over and tell Hal the news. I've violated my parole already."

"What time is it?" inquired Mrs. Overton.

"A quarter to six!"

"And, good gracious!" cried the little woman, jumping up from her chair. "Hal, in a few minutes more your father will be home, and not a blessed move has been made toward supper. There's no time to get anything ready now. Hal, I shall have to send you around the corner to the delicatessen shop, although I hate such ready-made meals."

"Mother," demanded Hal, with a pretense at mild astonishment, "would you think of sending a commissioned officer in the United States Army around on errands, with packages to bring home?"

"I—I guess that wouldn't be just right, would it?" agreed Mrs. Overton. "Never mind, my boy. I'll run right around myself. It will take me some time to get used to all the dignity that goes with your new position."

"You needn't bother to go, Mother," laughed Hal. "An officer who would let his mother run errands to save his own dignity would be sure to come to a bad end in the Army. I was only joking, of course. This is a day to celebrate, so I propose to ask you and father to dine out this evening. There are several good places in town."

"Which one do you prefer?" broke in Lieutenant Noll quickly.

"Ralston's," Hal replied. "There's music there, and the food and service are fine."

"Then I'll hurry home now and bring my folks up there, too, if I can," proposed Noll.

"Good!" agreed Hal.

"What hour, Mrs. Overton?" asked Noll, turning to that good woman.

"Ask Hal."

"In the Army it is customary to ask the ladies, Mother," Hal explained.

"Seven o'clock, then," said Mrs. Overton.

"Seven it shall be," nodded Noll. "That is, if I don't fail in coaxing Father and Mother out to dine."

"You won't fail," Mrs. Overton assured him. "They'll be proud enough to go out with you to-night."

Hal's father came home soon after. For years a clerk in one of the local stores, Mr. Overton had lately been promoted to be manager of the store. He was a quiet, thoughtful, studious man, and would probably have gone much higher in the world had not years of ill health interfered with his ambitions.

"I don't need to tell you how glad I am, young man," said the elder Overton quietly, when he had heard the afternoon's news. "Nor am I going to offer you any parental advice. Your record in the Army, so far, makes me feel sure that you will go on in the way you have begun, and that your record, at any point, will have been an honorable one. And now I must leave you and go upstairs to put on my best clothes in honor of the distinction that has come upon my son."

Just before seven the Overtons were seated at a table in Ralston's locally famous restaurant. Noll and his parents arrived at about the same moment. But the news had flown ahead of the young men. Just as the party was seating itself the orchestra crashed out into the strains of "See, the conquering hero comes!"

"I suppose that's meant for a joke on us," grinned Lieutenant Noll, in an undertone.

"Then try to look unconscious," returned Hal, in an equally low voice, and immediately engaged Noll's father and mother in conversation.

There was some whispering between waiters and patrons of the place, and presently a light sound of applause rippled out. It soon became a steady salvo.

Still the two young lieutenants went on with their chatting. But the leader of the orchestra had a further surprise. Giving his men only a moment for rest, he once more waved his violin bow, and the musicians started in with "The Star-Spangled Banner."

10

No soldier may ignore that splendid air; no citizen has a right to.

As the strain died out the young soldiers and their party re-seated themselves, going on with their chat again.

A waiter dropped two menu cards on the table, then stood waiting for the order.

"Won't the ladies select the dinner?" asked Hal.

"We'd prefer that our sons do that," smiled Mrs. Terry.

"You do it, then, Hal," directed Noll Terry. "I left my spectacles at home."

"What about officers and their duty to tell the truth?" chided Mrs. Terry, whose heart was full of joy and pride to-night.

"I'll amend my statement," replied Noll meekly. "I didn't bring my spectacles with me. But Hal ought to do the ordering, anyway. He always did. He was my ranking sergeant, and now he's my ranking lieutenant."

"We don't know that yet," objected Hal quickly. "We don't yet know anything about the order in which we passed."

"In the meantime," hinted Mr. Overton, "the cook's fire is running low."

So Hal turned his attention to the menu card, ordering with a free hand.

"Gracious! How many do you think there are at this table, young man?" demanded his mother.

"There are six of us," Hal answered. "But we can take hours in which to finish the meal, if we want to. Ralston's doesn't close until midnight."

The waiter, having received the order in silence, shuffled off without a word.

"Nothing very magnetic about that waiter," thought Hal, his glance following the waiter for an instant. "Somehow, his face looks familiar, too, but I've been away from home during the very few years when every boy turns into a young man. If I ever knew the chap I've forgotten him."

There was a rustling of silken skirts, then a resolute and very important-looking woman paused at the table. Just behind her waited a short, thin, rather negative-looking man.

The woman was red-faced, despite the liberal amount of powder with which she had striven to conceal the fact. She was richly dressed, and wore a few jewels, though not really enough of them to violate good taste. Hal recognized her as a Mrs. Redding, who, thanks largely to her husband's inherited wealth, had succeeded in making herself one of the leaders of local society. Mr. Redding was known principally as "Mrs. Redding's husband."

"Just a moment, my dear Mrs. Overton," cried Mrs. Redding cordially. "And you, too, my dear Mrs. Terry! I am pausing only a moment to congratulate you on the splendid news. I can well imagine how proud you are of your sons. And I must congratulate these two very distinguished sons, also."

Hal and Noll had risen promptly, though gravely and without haste. They bowed their acknowledgment of the congratulations.

"And how long are you going to be with us?" asked Mrs. Redding, allowing her gaze to wander from the face of one young officer to the other's.

"We don't know, madam," Hal replied courteously. "We are still in ignorance as to our orders."

11

"I shall hope to see much of you both, and of your families," Mrs. Redding beamed graciously. "To-morrow afternoon Mr. Redding and I, with some of our friends, are going to motor down the river in our new cruising boat, dining at the club-house. We should be delighted if you would accompany us. You won't disappoint us, will you?"

Hal glanced at his mother, who offered no reply, but glanced back at her son.

"We are very grateful for your invitation, Mrs. Redding," Lieutenant Hal continued. "Terry and I feel that we are not in the least certain about being able to keep any engagements that we might make, since we are both awaiting orders from the War Department. Besides all my engagements are in the charge and keeping of my mother."

"Then you will accept for yourself and friends, won't you, my dear Mrs. Overton?" asked Mrs. Redding, again turning to Hal's mother.

"I—I am very much afraid that we can't go to-morrow afternoon," replied Mrs. Overton slowly.

"Oh, well, then, we will make a later appointment," smiled Mrs. Redding affably. "There will be plenty of time, I am sure. So glad to have seen you this evening."

Still smiling, Mrs. Redding swept on through the restaurant with Mr. Redding in her wake. Somehow, one instinctively felt sorry for Mr. Redding; he looked very much like a small boat towing astern of a larger craft.

"I am wondering very much," smiled Hal's mother. "Although we have gone to the same church for the last fifteen years, Mrs. Redding has never before seemed to know who I am. She is suddenly very cordial."

"That is because you now have a son who is an officer in the Army," interposed Noll's father. "An Army officer is supposed to be a man of some social consequence."

"But that doesn't give me any more social consequence. I'm just the same woman that I always was," objected Mrs. Overton sensibly.

"But at least, my dear," suggested Hal's father, "you will be visiting your son at his post one of these days, and he may also urge you to bring some of your women friends."

"I certainly shall," Hal agreed.

"And Mrs. Redding may feel that she would like to be one of the invited," continued the elder Overton. "So, my dear, you see that you will become of social consequence. Others than Mrs. Redding, who have never even bowed to you before, will now be calling on you."

"I don't want new friends of that sort," remarked Hal's mother quietly.

"My dear, you'll have to be very agile if you expect to dodge all such new friends," laughed Hal's father.

Since Hal had given the order the orchestra had played several numbers. All of the little dining party were now becoming rather impatient for dinner.

"I guess our waiter doesn't like us very well," half-grumbled Lieutenant Hal.

"Very likely," nodded his father. "Of course you recognized the waiter."

"I can't say, sir, that I did."

12

"The waiter is Bunny Hepburn, more than three years older than when you last saw him," replied Mr. Overton.

"Bunny Hepburn? The son of that anarchist who spouts about man's rights in beer-gardens?" questioned Hal. "Hepburn the man who is always trying to start strikes and labor riots?"

"That's the man, and Bunny is a half-worthy son of the sire, I hear," replied Mr. Overton.

"Here comes Bunny now," announced Mr. Terry.

Bunny appeared, setting bread and butter on the table, distributing knives, forks and spoons at the places and filling the water glasses.

"Will you bring the first course of our dinner right along now, waiter?" Hal asked pleasantly.

"When I can," came the half surly reply. "You'll have to wait your turn with the other customers."

"We expect to do that," Hal agreed, without resentment. "But we've been waiting about forty minutes now, and many others have been served who came in since we did."

"You needn't think you're running this restaurant," sneered the waiter.

"By no means," Hal agreed. "But we are at least paying for our food, for attendance and civility."

"You'll get all the attendance you're entitled to," grumbled the waiter. "Don't think you own the earth. Soldiers are no good."

"A lot of people entertain that opinion," Hal answered quietly, turning his back on the impudent waiter.

All might still have gone well, had Bunny been content to drop it there. But, as readers of the first volume in this series, "Uncle Sam's Boys in the Ranks," are aware, Bunny had been bred in contempt of the military and of everything connected with it.

"You soldiers are nothing but just a lot of cheap skates," Bunny muttered on bitterly. "You wear a uniform that is nothing but the cheap livery of slavery to the wealthy, and march under a flag that stands for nothing but tyranny to the poor and down-trodden of humanity."

This was almost word for word a copy from the anarchistic speeches of Bunny's father.

Lieutenant Hal's face went white as he wheeled once more in his chair and rose quickly.

Mrs. Overton had a momentary notion that her son was going to knock Bunny down, and she wouldn't have blamed him if he had. But Bunny quailed somewhat before the blazing light in the young Army officer's eyes.

"Stand back, waiter," ordered Hal quietly. Then, looking very tall and dignified, Lieutenant Hal stepped across the restaurant, going over to the desk, where the proprietor stood chatting with the cashier.

"Are you being properly served?" inquired Mr. Ralston, who had learned who this young guest was.

"Not especially. I have no personal complaint to make against the waiter, but I shall feel greatly obliged if you can send us a different man to wait on us."

"With pleasure," replied Mr. Ralston promptly. "But you will be doing me a genuine service, Mr. Overton, if you will tell me in what way the present waiter has offended you."

"He didn't offend me personally," Hal replied quietly, "but he spoke disrespectfully of the Flag I serve, and the uniform I am proud to wear."

"Thank you very much. Will you tell me what the waiter said?"

Hal repeated the words accurately.

"I will send you another waiter, Mr. Overton, and will see to it personally that you are not again annoyed. I thank you for having reported the matter to me."

Hal returned to his seat. Bunny had already vanished behind the swinging doors at the rear. Mr. Ralston followed him out into the cook's domain.

"Peterson, I want you to wait on Mr. Overton's party," called Mr. Ralston, whereat Bunny started slightly. "And, Peterson, I want you to serve and attend to their wants in your best style."

"Yes, sir," replied Peterson, an older waiter.

"Chef," continued the proprietor, "you will see to it that the delayed dinner for the Overton party is served ahead of anything else, and in your best style. Hepburn, come here!"

Bunny approached, a defiant scowl on his sulky face.

"Hepburn, I am told that you grossly insulted the Flag and the Army uniform."

"I didn't," retorted Bunny, "but I won't allow any of them tin-soldier dudes to put it over me."

"Your present language sufficiently justifies the charge made against you," replied Mr. Ralston quietly. "This restaurant is intended as a resort for ladies and gentlemen, and all right-minded persons respect our Army and Navy and those who serve their country."

"I'll tell you, right now, I hain't got any respect for them tin-soldiers," retorted Bunny defiantly.

"That will be all, Hepburn. Get out of here!"

With that the proprietor turned on his heel, leaving the cook's domain. Bunny was white with wrath. He tried to talk to some of the other employes present, but none of them paid any attention to him.

No effort did young Hepburn make to get his street clothes until the head waiter brought him back an envelope containing his wages.

"I'll remain here until I see you get out," remarked the head waiter coldly.

"You may wait a long time," sneered Bunny.

"No, I won't. If you're not out of here in a hurry I'll help you through the back door."

Not until then did Bunny Hepburn realize that he was actually discharged.

"Get out now," ordered the head waiter, looking as if he would be glad of an opportunity to help the discharged one through the back door.

"Oh, all right. I'll git," snarled Bunny Hepburn, thrusting on his hat and slouching out through the door. "But I'll get even with that cheap Army officer in short order!"

Like some other inconsequential fellows of his class, Bunny was usually a man of his word in matters of revenge.

CHAPTER III

ROWDY VERSUS REGULAR

AFTER a pleasant evening Hal and Noll escorted their parents homeward at somewhere around half-past ten o'clock.

Both young soldiers, however, were still so full of the day's news and so wide awake that neither felt at all like turning in for sleep as yet. So they met immediately afterward for a slow stroll through the streets on this warm summer evening.

"Where shall we go?" asked Hal, as the chums met.

"I don't care," Noll answered. "One set of streets will do as well as another."

"We'll take pains, anyway, to keep on the well-lighted streets," Hal proposed smilingly. "It wouldn't do for two poor, lonely soldiers to go into any of the darker quarters where danger may lurk."

"Tell you what we'll do then," offered Noll.

"We'll get a policeman to walk around with us and protect us from harm."

"Now let us have done with fooling for a little while, Noll. I remember something that Prescott was telling me once."

"*Lieutenant* Prescott," Terry interrupted quietly.

"Guess again, chum. You forget that we have been lieutenants since—well, since four o'clock this afternoon. So I am within my rights in simply calling him by his last name."

"True," admitted Noll. "I've been in the ranks so long that, somehow, it seems hard to realize that I am suddenly an officer, and the equal of any other second lieutenant in the Army."

"Prescott was telling me," went on Hal, "of a great friend he and Holmes had at West Point. He was a young Virginian, Anstey by name. Now Prescott and Holmes both feel as though they'd gladly give their left hands for a chance to grip Anstey's paw; yet since leaving West Point Prescott and Holmes have not laid eyes on Anstey—which brings me up to the question: How are we going to feel if you and I are constantly serving on different sides of the earth from each other?"

Lieutenant Noll Terry looked almost startled.

"By Jove, I hadn't thought of that," he muttered.

"I've been thinking of it," Hal rejoined. "Now, Noll, what is the matter with you and me drawing up a request, both signing it, asking that, if in accordance with military interests, we be assigned to the same regiment and battalion?"

"To whom should such a request go?"

"To the adjutant general of the Army, I imagine, since neither of us as yet belongs to any regiment or department."

"Won't the adjutant general put us down as the two original, very cheeky shave-tails?" wondered Noll.

"That's a chance we'll have to take. Though if we make what seems a perfectly proper request, and in a wholly respectful manner, I don't see how the adjutant general can find fault with two inexperienced young officers, even if our request be a rather unusual one."

"If you get up the paper I'll sign it with you," agreed Noll, without a moment's further hesitation.

"I'll prepare that paper the first thing in the morning," promised Hal. "Whew, but I wish we had even an inkling of what our first duty is to be."

"Anywhere in 'God's country'" (in Army parlance, 'God's country' means the United States), replied Noll. "I don't want to see the Philippines again inside of a year."

For longer than they realized the two chums strolled the streets, now grown very quiet as the hour was late for a small city. Indeed, the two new lieutenants paid little heed to their course. So, after a while, they reached the rougher parts of the town.

Bunny Hepburn, having gone away from the restaurant with his heart full of hate, had fallen in with a group of companions of his own sort. These young men had visited beer-gardens and other places of low repute. Bunny's companions were the human fruits of his father's peculiar teachings. For the most part these young fellows were "professional labor men" of the lowest type. None of them ever worked long or steadily at anything, except with their tongues. They were a gross libel on the real workingmen of the country—the steady, sober, industrious toilers who are the real backbone of the country.

Bunny's companions, instead, were of a sort who hang upon the words of such speakers and agitators as the elder Hepburn. While disliking industrial work, and resorting to it only when there was no other choice as against starvation, these young fellows were always on hand in times of strike or riot, ready for any violence and seldom hesitating at extortion or pillage when the chance presented itself.

"I tell you, fellows," Bunny proclaimed hoarsely, "I'm going to get square with that tin-soldier dude, Overton. I hear he's been made an officer in the Army to-day. He feels bigger than all outdoors! He made a kick that cost me the best job I ever had."

"Imagine Bunny working!" jeered one of the crowd.

"That was the beauty of the job," snarled Bunny. "It wasn't real work. It was more like belonging to a club. I had to stand around a little, and pass things, and so forth. But I got fifteen a month, my meals, and three or four dollars a day in tips."

"I don't blame you, then, for being sore at losing the job," remarked another young "labor" man of Bunny's own stripe. "That kind of job was a good deal like easy graft."

"That's just what it was," rejoined Bunny feelingly. "And I lost it all on account of that—*Say, fellows!*"

This last appeal Bunny whispered hoarsely. Then he pointed ahead down the street.

"Here comes that soldier-loafer, Overton, now. And his friend with him."

"Now's your chance to take it out, Bunny!" prodded one of the gang.

"Fellows," declared Bunny earnestly, "it's the chance for all of us to take it out of that pair! Think how often the regulars have fired into honest, hard-working men!"

By that designation Bunny referred to rioters.

"There's two of them, and they hain't got no guns or bayonets this time," Bunny Hepburn continued hoarsely. "How many are there of us?"

"Twelve," replied another, "not counting Skinny Carroll."

"Skinny can work at his old game of lookout," muttered Bunny. "Get busy, Skinny."

Skinny was an undersized, weazened little fellow, with a large, badly-shaped head and an extremely bright pair of keen, fox-like eyes. Many a time had he been lookout against the coming of the police, while stronger, harder-handed companions carried out some piece of violence against law and order.

With a chuckle Skinny promptly turned and fled to the next corner, where he could watch four ways at once.

Bunny's companions found themselves committed to a new deed before they quite realized it.

"My pop has often told you fellows all about the soldiers," went on Bunny quickly. "Now, we've got a chance to settle one score for labor. We'll sail into that pair like a ton of brick. Use 'em up! Don't be gentle, or turn faint-hearted! Remember, there's enough of us to swear to a good 'frame-up' if this thing gets into court. Don't be chicken-hearted or white-livered! Line up, the bunch of you!"

Hal and Noll, as they strolled along the side street, saw the little group ahead. It was an unimportant street, devoted to business in the day-time. Neither of the Army boys distinguished Bunny, who kept himself well concealed behind the other idlers until Hal and Noll had reached the gang. Then Bunny threw himself forward.

"Yah! yah!" he snarled. "Get me thrown out of me job, will you, you soldier-loafer!"

"Hullo, it's Bunny!" cried Hal, recognizing the speaker.

"Yep! It's me—Bunny Hepburn!" jeered the ex-waiter. "But you won't know what your name is when I get through with you!"

"Bosh!" rejoined Hal, rather impatiently. "Step aside. Don't block the sidewalk. It's broad enough for us all!"

"You don't sneak out of it that easy!" jeered Bunny.

"Behave yourself, and let me by," requested Hal Overton sternly.

He tried to push the noisy fellow out of his path. Bunny, with the strength of the gang behind him, swung a hard blow at the Army boy's face.

In self-defense Hal Overton was obliged to fend off the blow. But Bunny came back at him again.

"Sail into the soldier-loafers!" called Bunny.

Wolf-like, the gang attacked in a pack, and on all sides at once. It didn't take Noll Terry an instant to see that this was serious business. Without a word Noll sprang back to back with Hal, and thus they met the onslaught.

In the crowd there were some hard-hitters, and the odds were tremendous.

On the other hand, Hal and Noll were no mean boxers. They had gained their skill with their fists in many a brisk garrison bout with the gloves. Moreover, both Army boys possessed the advantage of soldierly courage and discipline.

So, for a few moments, though they took some blows, yet they managed to keep off the wolf-pack fairly well.

Hal Overton's blood was up now, and he was dangerous. Watching his chance he let fly a blow that caught Bunny forcefully on the nose.

"Wow-ow-ow! O-o-oh!" wailed Bunny, trying to find shelter behind one of his companions. "The soldier-loafer is trying to kill me. Wade into him, fellers! Get him down and——"

At that moment Hal, with Noll at his back, worked through the line and caught Bunny over his left eye with a force that sent the noisy one down to the sidewalk.

"Get up, you cur!" ordered Hal.

For a moment the members of the gang on Overton's side of the fight seemed paralyzed.

Gripping Bunny Hepburn by the collar, Hal dragged the fellow to his feet and instantly planted a blow that closed the other eye.

"Now, you'll stay put," panted Hal breathlessly. "Come on, the rest of you hyenas, and we'll walk through the whole crowd of you!"

With a yell of defiance the gang closed in. While the mix-up was at its hottest, a low, trilling whistle sounded from Skinny Carroll's lips. Only two of the gang heard it in the excitement; that pair took to their heels at once.

Down the street came a pair of flying feet.

"Cop! cop!" yelled Skinny Carroll. "Duck and run!"

Three more of the gang heard and took to their heels at once. One of the fugitives ran squarely into the policeman's arms. The blue-coat stopped another by drawing his revolver and commanding a halt. When the policeman came along with his two prisoners Noll had a third to add to the collection. Hal had Bunny and another of the late fighting crew.

"What's this trouble about?" demanded the policeman gruffly.

"It's an outrage, and high time you got here," wailed Bunny. "Officer, just look at me!"

"You seem to look just right to me," grinned the policeman.

"Officer, I demand that you arrest these two fellows!" insisted Bunny, in a shaking voice. "They'd have killed me if you hadn't got here just when you did."

"Hold your tongue," commanded the policeman. Then, turning to Hal, he asked:

"What's the rights of this affair?"

"Don't you listen to what they say!" screamed Bunny. "They'll lie like a house afire. I was going along, minding my own business, when this pair jumped on me. You see what they did to me."

"Officer, what's the meaning of this?" demanded a man who had just come on the scene. It was Bunny's father, the agitator and anarchistic lecturer.

"If you'll keep quiet long enough I'll soon find out," retorted the policeman.

"Officer," demanded the elder Hepburn, "do you know who I am?"

"Yes; that's why I want you to keep quiet," retorted the policeman, with no great show of awe or respect.

"But——"

"Get back and keep quiet until I've had time to look into this thing!" blazed the policeman ominously.

"Minion of the hireling law," began the elder Hepburn, running his fingers through his hair and striking an attitude.

"Hepburn, in the name of the Commonwealth, I demand your assistance in taking care of the prisoners," retorted the policeman grimly. "Disobey at your peril. Here, take charge of this prisoner," indicating Bunny. "If you let him escape you'll go to jail for it!"

Thus summoned in the name of the Commonwealth the elder Hepburn, though he loathed his task, had to play the part of a police officer or take the consequences. Hepburn, like his son, was noisy but not brave; he had no desire to serve his state in jail, so he served it on the street.

However, the arresting party and prisoners had gone only as far as the next corner when they encountered Chief of Police Blake, an official who was not afraid of any one or anything.

"What's this?" asked the chief.

Hal and Noll were asked to explain the affair, while the two Hepburns and Bunny's companions were forced, much against their will, to keep still.

"We don't care about pressing any charge, chief," Hal added. "This crowd got punished enough as it was."

"One of them certainly did," grinned Chief Blake, taking in the extent of damage done to Bunny's countenance.

"Chief, I insist that you arrest these two soldier-loafers!" cried Bunny hoarsely.

"And I back up that demand!" added the elder Hepburn, with what he considered impressive dignity.

"Bosh!" retorted Chief Blake. "I'd take the word of these two Army officers against a whole slumful of rowdies like these young fellows. And so would any judge in his right mind. I refuse to arrest either of these young Army officers, for I'm convinced that they acted only in their own defense."

"Officer," broke in the elder Hepburn dramatically, "you have no right to take the word of hireling soldiers against honest young working——"

"Go on! Chase yourselves! A quick vanish or a long night behind the hard iron bars!" cried Chief Blake, dropping into the language that Bunny and his companions could best understand. "Another piece of jaw, and to the green-lighted doorway you all go!"

Then, nodding to Hal and Noll to stroll along with him, Chief Blake left the discomfited trouble-makers.

"Another proof that the law exists only for the benefit of the favored few!" hissed Bunny's father. "But this latest outrage shall not go unnoticed. There are ways of getting justice, even under such a miserable government as ours, and we shall have recourse to those ways. Come with me, gentlemen, and I shall show you what can be done!"

There are always ways of making trouble when one is bound to do it. Moreover, Mr. Hepburn was an expert at trouble-making, and on this night he worked overtime.

There was trouble ahead, as the two Army boys discovered on awakening in the morning.

CHAPTER IV

A COURT OF INQUIRY ORDERED

THERE were two morning newspapers published in the town; or, as some people put it, "one and a quarter."

The *Tribune* appealed to the more orderly element in the community. In the *Tribune* was an account of the police version of the night before, to the effect that Bunny Hepburn and a gang had set upon Lieutenants Overton and Terry, of the Regular Army, and that the two young officers had given an excellent account of themselves in the encounter, afterwards declining to prosecute the gangsters.

The *Sphere*, the other morning sheet, made its appeal to the rougher element of the city. It was through this sheet that Orator Hepburn had been able to acquire much of his local notoriety. Hepburn and Sayles, the latter the proprietor of the *Sphere*, had been cronies for five years. To Sayles the older Hepburn had gone, taking along with him his "witnesses."

As was to be expected, the *Sphere* attacked the two young officers, giving wholly the Hepburn version of the affair.

"But this will not be the last of the matter," the *Sphere* proclaimed dramatically. "There are reliefs to be had from such outrages. Mr. Hepburn has already taken the matter up with a strong hand. Through the night two of our ablest local attorneys toiled at preparing the papers in the case. A formal complaint has been drawn up, backed by the testimony of the witnesses under oath, and all the papers in the case are now on their way to Washington. The residents of this city will soon be in a position to know whether such outrages may be safely committed by officers of our Regular Army, a body of men organized supposedly for the protection of the citizens of the country!"

"Well, wouldn't that blow your hat off?" demanded Lieutenant Noll, as he and his chum went over the account published by the *Sphere*.

"It's evidently aimed with a view to blowing our heads off," muttered Hal Overton.

"What talented liars there are in this world!" uttered Noll Terry, in high disgust.

"They wouldn't do so much harm, though, if it weren't for the fact that sometimes liars, under oath, manage to get themselves believed," returned Hal.

"Is anybody going to believe this rot?" insisted Noll.

"Some one in the War Department might, not knowing the local reputation of the Hepburns."

"Well, the War Department will know, if it takes any action on these trumped-up, lying charges," declared Lieutenant Noll hotly.

"Of course we won't lie down and tamely submit to such false charges," agreed Lieutenant Overton.

"Going out for a walk this morning?" Noll wanted to know.

"I feel much more inclined to sit here and think this whole thing over," Hal answered, pointing to the lying sheet.

"Hal, if we stay indoors to-day the *Sphere* will have it to-morrow that we are overwhelmed with shame and fear, and have kept in hiding."

"And, if we go out around the town," laughed Hal, "the *Sphere* will proclaim to-morrow that we are brazenly showing ourselves and trying to cheek down the charges against us."

"Then we'll take our choice and do as we please," remarked young Terry. "Come along out."

Hal got his hat, and the chums went forth, again in their tennis flannel undress.

The news had not been slow in spreading. They had gone hardly a block when they were stopped by friends, and congratulated on having taught Bunny such an effective lesson.

Others there were, however, who whispered behind the backs of the young officers. Hal and Noll were not slow to catch some of those whispers.

"We're a whole lot more important than we were three years ago," grinned Noll. "Now, at last, we seem to have the town divided into two camps concerning us."

"Three," corrected Hal.

"How do you make that out?"

"One crowd believes the charges against us, and another doesn't. The third crowd isn't sure, or doesn't care."

"One fellow I'm after, anyway," muttered Noll grimly.

"Who's that?"

"Sayles."

"Who's he?"

"Don't you know?"

"I'm afraid I can't recall a party named Sayles," Hal answered thoughtfully.

"Why, he's the pen-hoister who gets out the *Sphere*!"

"Oh, well, what are you going to do to him, Noll?"

"I'm going to make him prove all he printed in his lying sheet."

"He can—with the aid of the kind of witnesses that he has back of him," Hal reminded his chum.

"Well, we shall have to see if the testimony of such witnesses will 'go' in court," Noll contended grimly.

"Are you going to prosecute the fellow?"

"I'm going to sue Sayles for libel," Noll retorted.

"Is the fellow worth the trouble?" Hal inquired doubtfully.

"No, but our reputations are," rejoined Noll bluntly. "Hal, we are commissioned officers in the United States Army. If that means anything, it means that the United States government certifies us to the world to be

21

gentlemen as well as officers. You know the legal phrase, 'officer and gentleman.' If we lie down tamely, and submit to such libelous attacks as the *Sphere* made on us this morning, then we do a wrong to the whole body of officers and gentlemen in the Army. The officers of our service have always had to stand a lot of abuse from a certain kind of so-called newspapers. It's time to stop it by hitting any nail that shows its head. We owe it to our brother officers."

"Noll, I'm inclined to think you're right."

"I know I am. Come along, down this street."

"Where now?"

"I'm headed for the office of Lawyer Kimball. He's the best man in town to handle our case."

To the lawyer's office, therefore, the two Army boys went. Lawyer Kimball listened, nodded, accepted their case to do what he could with it, and offered them some advice.

Late that evening each Army boy received a telegram from the War Department, to the effect that a complaint had been lodged against them. They were ordered to remain in town, close to their home addresses, for the receipt of further orders.

Next morning the *Sphere* had much more to say, and said it jubilantly. It informed its readers that the War Department had taken up the matter and had promised to give satisfaction. There was a further bitter attack on Lieutenants Overton and Terry.

That afternoon Hal escorted his mother to one of the department stores, as Mrs. Overton had some purchases to make. They came face to face with Mrs. Redding. The latter woman started slightly and looked embarrassed. She would have gone by without bowing, but it was impossible for Mrs. Redding to pretend that she had not seen Mrs. Overton and her son.

"Good afternoon," said Mrs. Redding, in a low voice.

Hal lifted his hat gravely as the society woman hastened on.

"She wasn't as cordial as she was the other evening," remarked Mrs. Overton dryly.

"No, Mother; I'm afraid that Mrs. Redding doesn't care to risk going any further with our acquaintance until she knows whether I'm to continue in the Army."

"It won't be necessary for her to go any further," remarked Mrs. Overton cooly. "I don't wish to know her. I am satisfied with my present circle of friends."

"Old friends are always believed to be the best," murmured Hal.

The day after that meeting Hal and Noll each received word from the War Department, containing copies of the complaint, and stating that a court of inquiry would be ordered forthwith, and that the young officers would be informed of the time and place of the meeting of the court.

An officer, when placed formally under charges, is tried before a court-martial, whose members are officers of higher rank than the accused. A court of inquiry, on the other hand, may hear charges in the first instance, and on the finding of this preliminary court the War Department decides whether a court-martial shall be convened.

"You see, Noll, the Hepburns are going right through with their 'case,'" observed Lieutenant Overton.

"So are we," retorted Noll, pursing his lips. "And the best crowd will win."

"Or else the crowd whose witnesses won't hesitate to perjure themselves," Hal muttered.

As the Army boys had just been appointed officers, the immediate present was the best time for getting them out of the service if they were not worthy of places in it. So the War Department acts with unusual speed in such matters. Within a week from the time of receiving the complaint the court of inquiry, composed of three officers sent over from Army Headquarters in New York, was on the scene.

The mayor offered the court the use of one of the council chambers at the city hall, and the offer was accepted.

"We shall soon know," remarked the *Sphere*, "what the national government's idea of justice is. The culprits face their ordeal to-day!"

At nine o'clock that morning, in fact, Major Elbert, president of the court, rapped for order.

CHAPTER V

THE WAR DEPARTMENT SAYS ITS SAY

FOR witnesses Bunny had rounded up all of his gang of that notable night, with the one exception of Skinny Carroll. It would never do to have Carroll go on the stand and admit that he had been posted as a lookout.

Bunny and all his friends, under the coaching of a local lawyer, had proved themselves expert perjurers.

Even Major Elbert, president of the court, before that body had been in session for an hour, looked as though he believed the case a dark one against the young officers.

The elder Hepburn was on hand. He tried hard to palm off one of his pet orations on the court, but Major Elbert shut him off sternly.

Not one of Bunny's crew told the truth. That wasn't what they were there for.

Hal and Noll attended court, as required, in dress uniform. It was the first time that they had worn these handsome service garments officially, and it seemed a pity that they should have to wear them under such circumstances.

At last Hal was sworn. He told the truth, briefly, clearly, accurately. Then a shady lawyer engaged by the Hepburns undertook to cross-examine the young lieutenant. Hal's testimony was not to be shaken in the slightest detail. The lawyer resorted to abuse, but Hal kept his temper. Major Elbert took a hand, warning the lawyer that he must keep his speech within the limits of gentlemanly use.

Noll went on the stand and told his story. It did not differ from Hal's in any detail, nor was young Terry to be shaken by cross-examination.

Still it was the testimony of two witnesses against that of a dozen witnesses.

Then the policeman who had interfered was called to the stand. He had not witnessed the affray, and so could give no testimony as to whether Lieutenant Overton or Bunny Hepburn had started the affair.

Chief Blake followed.

"Do you know anything of the affray itself?" questioned Major Elbert.

"Nothing," admitted the chief.

The Hepburn lawyer settled back in his chair with a dark look of satisfaction.

"In what way, Chief," queried the major, "do you feel that you can aid this court in arriving at a proper decision?"

"I am here, sir, to testify, if desired, to the characters borne by the complainants and by the defendants."

Chief Blake then went on to state that he had known Lieutenants Overton and Terry for many years, with the exception of the time that they had been absent serving in the Regular Army. The chief stated that the character of each young man was above reproach.

"What do you know regarding any of the complaining witnesses?" inquired Major Elbert.

"I object!" shouted the Hepburn lawyer, rising.

"To what do you object?" inquired the major mildly, glancing at the lawyer. "To having the characters of the complaining witnesses stated?"

"We object, may it please the court, on the ground that the chief of police is not qualified to express a competent opinion."

"We will hear what Chief Blake has to say," decided the president of the court, "and we will pass on the value of his evidence later on."

"'Bject!" snapped the lawyer.

"Be good enough, sir, to sit down!"

Chief Blake began his statement by explaining that the elder Hepburn had been for years a notorious local character——

"'Bject!" shouted the lawyer.

"Sit down, sir"—from the president of the court.

Chief Blake continued his testimony, producing copies of official records to show that the elder Hepburn had been four times arrested for inciting disorder and on similar complaints.

"'Bject!"

"Orderly," called Major Elbert. A sergeant who had accompanied the officers of the court stepped forward. "Orderly," continued the major, mildly, "if this attorney makes any further disturbance, put him out of the room. You should understand, Counsellor, that this is a military court, and that you, as a civilian attorney, are admitted here as a matter of courtesy. The chief of police will now go on with his testimony, and if there be anything in it, Counsellor, to which you wish to take exception, at the proper time you will be afforded an opportunity. But we cannot have the court's time wasted by boisterous conduct on the part of any one present."

Major Elbert's manner was not that of the bully, or of one abusing brief authority. His voice was mild and soft, but he meant business.

24

Chief Blake continued, testifying that not one of the young fellows in Bunny's crew was a valuable or reliable member of the community. Four of them had been arrested on minor charges in the past, and all of them, Bunny included, had given the police of the town many kinds of trouble and annoyance in the past.

"Chief," inquired the major softly, "what do you feel at liberty to say regarding the truthfulness of any of the complaining witnesses?"

"I wouldn't believe one of 'em, sir, under any oath that could be imposed on 'em," replied Chief Blake bluntly. "In the past my policemen and I have known every one of that outfit to lie repeatedly when accused of different kinds of disorderly conduct."

"Then you believe, Chief, that the complaining witnesses are members of a definite gang, and that they are all wholly untruthful and undependable?"

"To that question, sir, I have no hesitation whatever in saying 'yes.'"

"Have you any more evidence to offer, Chief?"

"I have two witnesses outside, sir, whom I think you would like to hear."

"Will you send for them?"

Bunny and his crew, during the testimony of Chief Blake, which had not been expected by them, had felt partly dazed. They sat either scowling or grinning sheepishly while the new witnesses were being awaited. The elder Hepburn sat behind the younger men, running the fingers of his right hand through his glossy black hair.

When the two witnesses entered, the gangsters started and exchanged glances. One was a middle-aged man, the other Skinny Carroll.

"This gentleman," announced Chief Blake, "is Mr. Robert Enwright. Mr. Enwright's store is at the corner below the scene of the affray now being investigated. Mr. Enwright sometimes sleeps over his store. He did during the night of the fight. He was awakened by hearing this other witness, Carroll, shout a warning that the police were coming. Mr. Enwright looked out of the window and recognized Carroll. So Mr. Enwright notified me, the next day, and I gathered Carroll in. Carroll finally admitted that he had belonged to the Hepburn gang, and that he had shouted a warning to his mates."

Mr. Enwright was then sworn, and substantiated Chief Blake's remarks. Next Skinny Carroll, nervously avoiding the black looks of Bunny and his crew, came forward and was sworn. He told the truth, now, as glibly as Bunny's friends had lied.

"Then, on that night, and at the time of the fight, you did act as lookout for young Hepburn and his friends?" asked Major Elbert.

"Sure," agreed Skinny readily.

"Who told you to act as lookout?"

"Bun Hepburn himself!"

"'Bject!" shouted the Hepburn lawyer.

The sergeant moved over and laid a hand on the attorney's shoulder.

"At what period in the affair," inquired the major, "were you so instructed to run up to the corner to act as a lookout against the coming of the police?"

"Just before de gang closed in," declared Skinny.

"Closed in—for what?"

"T' soak Overton and Terry."

"Then the gang did deliberately combine to waylay and attack Lieutenant Overton and Terry?"

"Surest pipe you ever lit," affirmed Skinny Carroll, in the only style of speech of which he was master.

The Hepburn attorney was then given an opportunity to cross-examine the police witnesses. He did not, however, succeed in shaking any of the testimony.

Within ten minutes more the inquiry was declared closed. Army courts do not announce their findings, which are sent, sealed, to the War Department, there to be acted upon as the President of the United States directs.

"We Shall See!"

For that reason Hal and Noll knew nothing of the nature of the court's findings. Both young lieutenants, however, looked decidedly cheerful as they left the city hall. Skinny Carroll went away under the protection of Chief Blake. The gang melted quickly, Bunny with them, but the elder Hepburn was found down by the gate, ready to fix the two Army boys with one of his dramatic glares.

27

"Probably you two *gentlemen* think you have cleared yourselves," sneered the orator. "You feel that you have squared the court and have killed my son's case. But we shall see!"

Hal, for answer, looked straight into Hepburn's eyes with a cold stare of contempt. Noll did not even trouble himself to glance at the fellow.

Four days later the Army boys received long official envelopes from the War Department. The findings of the court of inquiry had vindicated and exonerated both young officers, who would continue to enjoy the full confidence of the President and of the War Department. Further, Lieutenants Overton and Terry were authorized to publish this letter in any way that they chose.

The next morning the *Tribune* published the letters and congratulated the Army boys.

On the other hand, the *Sphere* printed a long screed against the government, and against the War Department in particular, and hinted that all Army officers, young and old, stood together in cases like the present one.

Before the day was over, however, Proprietor and Editor Sayles was having his own troubles. He had been summoned to Lawyer Kimball's office, where he discovered that he was about to be defendant in two suits for libel.

"But you can attack public officers in the press," retorted Sayles.

"Only as to their performance of their public duties," rejoined Counsellor Kimball. "You have grossly libeled my two clients in their private life. As they are Army officers, and therefore men of the highest standing as to honor, they can obtain a verdict for large damages."

Sayles tried to bluster, whereupon the lawyer advised him to seek an attorney of his own for consultation. Within a week Sayles knew more about the libel law, and gladly settled out of court to avoid the danger of having to pay much more after standing suit. The amount that he paid was five thousand dollars, and to do this the editor had to put a mortgage on his newspaper plant.

"Five thousand dollars is a nice little pile," remarked Noll, when the Army boys had been summoned to their attorney's office.

"As you have informed me that you regard Sayles's money as soiled, and that you will not use it for yourselves," continued the Counsellor, "I shall stick to my original agreement, which was not to charge you anything for my services unless the case had to go to court. Have you thought how you will apply this money?"

"Yes," came promptly from Noll. "In this town there are eighteen churches, one synagogue and one hospital. That makes twenty organizations in all. Mr. Kimball, will you send each of them your check for two hundred and fifty dollars?"

"Too bad you can't send the donations in Sayles's own name," laughed Lieutenant Hal.

"I can forward the sum to each recipient anonymously," replied the lawyer, his eyes twinkling, "and can state that Mr. Sayles is responsible for the gift."

When Editor Sayles, of the *Sphere*, received the thanks of eighteen churches, a synagogue and the hospital his face expressed helpless fury rather than good-will toward men.

CHAPTER VI

A SEND-OFF FROM THE "SPHERE"

HAL OVERTON came into the parlor, a few days later, to find his mother studying a pair of visiting cards.

"I was out, a little while ago, and found these cards under the door when I returned," explained Mrs. Overton, handing the cards to her son.

"Mr. and Mrs. Redding," Hal read from the pasteboards. "Shall you return their call, Mother?"

"I don't believe I shall. But you have something there to show me?"

"Yes; I met the postman on the street, and he handed me a letter—from the War Department."

"Your orders?"

"Yes, Mother."

"What regiment? Where are you to be stationed?" asked Mrs. Overton eagerly.

"Which question shall I answer first, Mother?" the Army boy queried, half-teasingly.

"Your station!"

"Fort Butler."

"Where on earth is that?"

"In Texas, on the border."

"Thank goodness, it's in the United States," exclaimed Mrs. Overton fervently. "I was afraid you'd be sent back to the Philippines, or to Guam."

"The Navy garrisons the island of Guam, Mother."

"Well, then, to Alaska, or to some other outlandish place. I'm glad you're to go to some place where I can get on the cars and go to see you."

There was to come a time in the no distant future when her splendid son would be called upon to go where she could not follow—a time when Hal and his associates would be over-seas fighting for the democracy of the world, as well as for the existence of their beloved homeland.

"And some of my first savings as an officer will go to pay your fare, Mother. But you don't seem interested in the regiment, after all."

"Well, which regiment is it?"

"The Thirty-seventh Infantry, Colonel Wheatman."

"Would you rather have gone to the Thirty-fourth?"

"For many reasons, much rather. But I'm contented to go wherever Uncle Sam sends me. That's the only right way for a soldier to feel."

"I would have liked the Thirty-fourth better, too," remarked Mrs. Overton thoughtfully. "The Thirty-fourth is soon due to be back from the Philippines, while your new Thirty-seventh may just be getting ready to start there."

"And the last bit of my news, Mother, is that I am to report for duty with my new regiment on September fifteenth."

"So soon?" cried Mrs. Overton, her voice keen with disappointment. "Why, it seems as though you had come home only yesterday. And now you must run away again."

"All in the soldier's game. But it won't be long before you'll be coming out to visit me."

"You have no house on the post, and you won't have any place to keep me if I come, Hal."

"A bachelor officer, Mother, must be very attentive to the married women on the post. Then one of the married women will invite his mother to visit at her quarters."

"You don't have to *flirt* with married women, I hope?"

"Not so you could notice it, Mother," replied Lieutenant Hal gravely. "An officer, we are taught in the Army, is the descendant of the knight of old. So the officer must be careful to be always very respectful with all women. If he fails in that obligation his brother officers make his stay in the Army so disagreeable that he's glad to get out of the Army altogether."

"Is the whole regiment stationed at Fort Cutler?"

"Fort Butler, Mother. No; only the second battalion of the regiment. Major Tipton will be my immediate commanding officer. And now you'll excuse me, won't you?"

"You're going around to Noll's?"

"Yes. We made a request that we be assigned to the same battalion. I'm mighty anxious to know whether it has been convenient to grant our wish."

"Does Mr. Ad Interim have anything to with *that*?" demanded Mrs. Overton.

"I believe not," laughed Hal, then vanished through the doorway.

"Strange to me what complete fascination there can be about the Army," mused Mrs. Overton. "That boy of mine, now that he's ordered to join his regiment again, is wholly and unreasonably happy."

Noll had received his orders just before Hal arrived. Lieutenant Terry was also ordered to Fort Butler.

"There isn't a thing left that we can ask for!" exclaimed Hal contentedly.

"I hope we'll have as good luck with each step upward," beamed young Terry.

"There may come a time in our upward progress when we can't serve in the same regiment," warned Hal. "That will be when we become lieutenant-colonels. The present law allows but one lieutenant-colonel to a regiment, you know."

"Oh, as far as that's concerned, cheer up, chum," grinned Lieutenant Noll. "Before we get anywhere near as high as lieutenant-colonel we may each be occupying a two-by-six in a soldiers' cemetery."

"It would please the Hepburns and Sayles better if we did now," laughed Hal. "But let's forget malice toward others—we've been able to get everything on earth that we've wanted so far. Noll, to-morrow morning, we must pay another visit to Sergeant Wright."

Several times since their return home the Army boys had been to call on Wright, a retired old Army sergeant living in this Jersey town. It was Sergeant Wright who had first inspired the boys with a desire for the Army life.

"We've got several visits to make, and very little time in which to do it," decided Noll.

It is difficult, indeed, to keep the press from learning all that is happening. The next morning the *Sphere* contained this paragraph:

"Most of our citizens will be glad to learn that Lieutenants Overton and Terry, of the Regular Army, are leaving soon to go to their new station in far-away Texas."

There was nothing libelous in that paragraph. It could be taken either way—as a piece of congratulation or as a covert sneer. So Hal and Noll concluded to let it pass as a joke, and each clipped out the paragraph to show at Fort Butler.

All the good home times ended at last. Divided between pangs of regret and eager thoughts of the new service as line officers, Hal and Noll boarded a train one morning and started west.

The new life, the goal of their youthful dreams, lay before them. What would it bring?

CHAPTER VII

AN OLD FRIEND IN A NEW GUISE

AT eleven o'clock on the morning of September fifteenth two slim, sun-burnt, erect and athletic-looking young men walked into headquarters at Fort Butler.

The sergeant seated at a desk in the outer room, after taking a look at them, concluded to take a chance. He rose, saluted and stood at attention.

"What can I do for you, gentlemen?" he asked.

"Is Major Tipton at headquarters?" queried Hal.

"Yes, sir."

"Will you take our cards in to the major if he is not too busily engaged to receive them?"

The sergeant glanced at the uppermost card, on which was printed, from engraved script, in the regular form for officers' cards:

"Henry Overton,
U. S. Army."

"At once, gentlemen," replied the sergeant. "Will you be seated!"

The sergeant vanished behind the door to the next room. In an instant he came out again, halting just beyond the doorway, and announced:

"Major Tipton wishes you to step inside, gentlemen."

Major Tipton was standing by his desk to receive his new young officers. He was a large man, tall, with broad shoulders and somewhat inclined to portliness. His hair was iron-gray, his face rather highly colored. But he looked the picture both of courtesy and heartiness as he held out a hand to Hal.

"Welcome, gentlemen," was his greeting. "Welcome to the Thirty-seventh. I can speak, with especial heartiness, for the second battalion."

Hal and Noll presented themselves by name.

"Be seated, gentlemen. And so you have come up from the ranks? We have many splendid officers in the service who took the same path to commissions. I had the hard-won pleasure of coming through West Point, but many of the officers who have served with me and under me came up from the ranks. Our battalion now has its full complement of officers. The two second lieutenants of the other companies are men just from West Point this year."

"I think you will like the post here, especially if you are fond of the water. As you will find, when you have time to take a walk, this reservation is right on the bank of the Rio Grande River. In fact, this post is a frontier station. But that you have already gathered from maps or other sources."

"We have looked up everything we could find about Fort Butler, sir," Noll answered.

"You are both bachelors, I understand."

"Yes, sir," assented Hal.

"Good. We have plenty of room in the bachelor quarters, and no more cottages, at present, for married officers. So, gentlemen"—here the major's eyes twinkled merrily—"you will be doing me an especial favor if you do not contemplate marriage for the present."

"We are wholly free from engagements in that line, sir." Noll laughed.

"I am glad to hear it, Mr. Terry. A young officer should first find out if he can live on his pay, before he tries to make it do for two persons. Having been informed that you were bachelor officers I have already given orders that your quarters be made ready. We have twelve sets of officer's quarters here, and, including yourselves, only five officers to put in the quarters. And now I take it that you will want to go to your quarters after your long ride on the train!"

"We are wholly at your orders, sir," responded Hal.

"Then I will take time to play host in what is really Uncle Sam's house. I will take you over to your quarters myself. Pardon me for a few moments, while I do some telephoning."

Calling up the quarters of Captain Goodale, Major Tipton said:

"Captain, this is the commanding officer. Your new second lieutenant, Mr. Terry, is here. He will call upon you at two o'clock this afternoon, unless you have another engagement for that time. Two is all right, is it? Thank you, Captain."

Major Tipton then called up Captain Foster, informing him that Mr. Overton would call upon him at two o'clock that afternoon.

"Now, where is your baggage, gentlemen? At the station, I suppose."

"Yes, sir."

"I will send for one of the battalion quartermaster sergeant's men to take your checks and have your baggage up here without delay."

A private soon entered, received the baggage checks of the young officers and departed.

"Now, come along, gentlemen," invited the major, reaching for his uniform cap. "I will take you over to your quarters at once."

Fort Butler looked like many another army post, in that the reservation was several hundred acres in extent; that it had well-laid, well-kept roads, a guard house, parade ground, hospital, administrative buildings, a barracks for enlisted men and other quarters for the officers. The post lay in a flat country bordering the river, and the grounds about the buildings were tastefully laid out.

32

From the little headquarters building Major Tipton led Hal and Noll in a somewhat southerly direction toward the officers' quarters. At the extreme western end of "officers' town" lay a plain, barracks-like building, with front porch upstairs and down.

"That barn will be your home, gentlemen," announced the major. "And the building just this side is the one that contains the officers' club."

"Officers' club," otherwise known as "officers' mess," is a term that might be misunderstood by a civilian. The "club" is where the bachelor officers eat their meals; other officers on post often eat there, too, especially in the absence of their families. There are reading and writing rooms at the "club," and other features that make it a somewhat pleasant lounging place for young officers in their few leisure hours. While there is plenty of comfort at an officers' club there are few in which anything like real luxury is to be found. And, while the civilian may remain at his club until well into the small hours the Army officer, with his next day of arduous duty ahead of him, usually leaves his club between nine and ten in the evening, if not much earlier.

Major Tipton then led the young officers to the bachelor house, explaining that he had assigned them quarters upstairs, as they would find them much pleasanter than the downstairs rooms.

The two sets of quarters proved to be facing each other, Hal's on the east side, Noll's on the west side. Each set consisted of a parlor and bedroom, with bath and dressing-room adjoining.

"There's room enough here, sir, to start married life in," smiled Lieutenant Overton.

"Have you that bee buzzing about you?" asked the major, giving him a keen glance.

"Not in the least, sir."

"I have arranged for two excellent men to act as your strikers," continued the commanding officer. "Their selection is, of course, subject to your approval. At Fort Butler an officer pays a striker eight dollars a month."

The two lieutenants expressed their thanks. While they were still inspecting their quarters two private soldiers came up with the baggage from the railway station.

"I'll take my leave, now, and give you time to dress," said the major, rising. "I shall be at the club during the noon-time to-day, and will introduce you to such of the officers as may be present."

Both young officers saluted as their commander withdrew.

"Now we've got to hustle," admonished Hal. "We'll have a lot to do."

"I'm busy," affirmed Noll, rising and making for the door to go to his own quarters.

Hardly had the door closed when a knock came. Another knock could be heard at Noll's door.

"Come in," called Hal, and a young private entered, saluting.

"Major Tipton arranged with me to serve as your striker, sir, until you make some other arrangement," reported the soldier.

"You've come at just the right moment, then," answered Hal. "Your name?"

"Ellis, sir."

"Very good, Ellis. Unpack my trunk and bags in the bedroom. I'm going into my bath."

"Very good, sir."

Catching up clean underclothing Lieutenant Hal retired to the bathroom. Completing his toilet with soldierly speed, the youthful lieutenant opened the door into his parlor.

Private Ellis arose, standing at attention.

Hal tarried only long enough to note that the striker had placed his swords in a corner, and that his revolver, belt and ammunition box lay on the desk.

"Ellis has done this sort of work before," Hal told himself. Then he stepped out, knocking on Noll's door. The latter's striker opened it at once.

"Lieutenant Terry is nearly ready, sir," reported Noll's striker.

An officer's striker is a species of military servant, yet it is not considered in the Army that the striker's work is really menial, or in any way degrading. Some of the best and brightest of the commissioned officers now serving in the Army have been employed in the past as strikers to officers. No private soldier is compelled to serve as striker. He does it only of his own choice, and is always paid by the officer, the amount of pay depending upon the extent and nature of the services so performed. A striker's work must not interfere with his performance of his own soldierly duties. A trained striker knows just the hours when he is expected to be at his officer's quarters, and just what he must do when he gets there.

Noll soon came out, presenting a striking sight in his brand-new, finely fitting uniform.

"I can't rid myself of the notion that I'm liable to arrest by the guard," laughed Noll as the chums made their way down the stairs.

"Why?" asked Hal.

"For daring to masquerade in an officer's uniform," grinned Noll.

"You'll get used to it soon," replied Hal. "You haven't been an enlisted man all your life, you know."

"But I have been during all the years that I've been really living," Noll retorted. "You look out, too, Hal, old bunkie, or you'll be saluting the first second lieutenant you see."

"I shall, anyway," Overton retorted. "Any other second lieutenant on the post, except yourself, ranks me, and I'm not sure but that you do."

Nor had the young lieutenants taken ten steps from their room when a soldier, turning the corner, brought his hand up to the visor of his cap in trim salute.

Hal was ready with his acknowledgment of the salute, but Noll started guiltily, half a second later, and hurriedly raised his own hand to return the soldier's courtesy.

"I was nearly caught that time," admitted Terry, in an undertone.

"Watch, out, chum. It's a grave matter, as you well enough know, for an officer to overlook a soldier's salute."

Three more soldiers passed them, but Noll was looking now, and fully alert to bring his own hand up to his cap.

Then the chums turned and ascended the steps to the club. Neither had ever before entered an officers' club, save on some errand of duty.

Major Tipton was waiting for them inside. There were two other officers present—First Lieutenants Johnson and Sears.

"Mr. Johnson is first lieutenant of F company, your company, Mr. Terry," stated the major. "Mr. Sears is first lieutenant of your company, H, Mr. Overton. These gentlemen, after luncheon, will take you to your respective captains and present you."

Soon there were sounds of others entering the hallway. Then a voice was heard, declaring firmly:

"You may think me a grind, but I have little sympathy with either officers or men who think too much of pleasure. The first duty of any soldier, from general down to rookie——"

Now three more officers stepped into the room.

"——is duty, and it should always be spelled with a capital 'D,'" finished the speaker earnestly.

Noll got a glimpse of that speaker. It startled him so that he drew back, muttering:

"For the love of Mike! It's our old Algy."

"Who?" queried Hal, who had not caught a glimpse, yet, of the face of the officer in question.

"It's Feathers—I mean, Ferrers," breathed Noll. "The officer who tried to resign because the Army was no place for a gentleman."

"Mr. Brisbane," sounded the major's voice, "I want you to meet a new officer, Mr. Overton. Mr. Pratt, Mr. Overton. Mr. Ferrers, Mr. ——"

"I think, Major, we have met before, sir," spoke Lieutenant Hal, turning to grasp the hand of Lieutenant Algy Ferrers, whom readers of "Uncle Sam's Boys as Sergeants" will well remember.

"Er—ah—yes," agreed Mr. Ferrers, but it was plain that his memory had deserted him as to Hal's face.

"Terry and I were sergeants at Fort Clowdry, Mr. Ferrers," Hal continued.

"Oh, I remember you now, of course," cried Algy heartily, but a slight flush mounted his cheeks at mention of Fort Clowdry.

Then Noll was presented to his brother officers.

Major Tipton withdrew, going to his own quarters just as luncheon was announced.

CHAPTER VIII

AT THE OFFICERS' CLUB

"WELL, it seems good to see old faces once more," said Algy, turning to the two new "youngsters," as younger officers are termed.

This was during a lull following a general conversation in which Hal and Noll had modestly refrained from taking any unnecessary part. "How did you leave every one in the old Thirty-fourth?"

"All the officers were well," Hal answered. "We lost several of our men who went down before Moro bullets, and disease got a few also."

"Then you've seen real service?" asked Algy Ferrers enviously.

"Yes; as much as the Moros could give us," nodded Noll. "Truth to tell, it was hard enough fighting to suit amateurs like us."

"Jove, I'd give a month's pay even to be able to fire a sentry's gun," declared Algy wistfully. "Ever since I left the Thirty-fourth I've been plugging away at the Service School at Fort Leavenworth."

"We didn't see you there in July," said Hal.

"No; in June I was ordered to this regiment."

"We had no notion of ever meeting you down here," replied Noll, now noting the figures, "37," just over the crossed rifles of Algy's collar device.

"I don't belong to this battalion," Ferrers explained. "I'm here temporarily, only, on special duty. I belong with B company, first battalion. I'm just praying for this regiment to be ordered somewhere where I can see some of the real fighting work."

"You will see fighting enough one of these days," said Hal prophetically.

"Cut that, Ferrers!" warned Sears. "Most of us are quite content with ordinary garrison routine in 'God's country.'"

"That's all well enough for you fellows," muttered Algy. "You don't need any of what I'm longing for. And I might have gone to the Philippines, too, with the Thirty-fourth, if I hadn't been such a dub," added Ferrers, glancing at Hal and Noll. "Perhaps I'm putting on airs, though. Overton, when I was at Fort Clowdry, I don't believe I was quite as high as a dub, was I?"

Algy spoke so plaintively that all the officers at table laughed.

"Oh, that's all right for you fellows," retorted Algy. "But you never had a glimpse of me in those old, first days. Why, fellows, I used to go off the post without permission. I got into an all-night party in Clowdry, and preferred it to reporting back in season to go on for guard duty."

A somewhat incredulous laugh from trained officers greeted this assertion.

"Oh, that's straight," declared Algy remorsefully. "And when Colonel North tried to do the fatherly act with me by way of remonstrance, I believe I assured him that my little lapse was nothing to get warm about."

A shout of genuine laughter greeted this reminiscence.

"And one day," pursued Algy, "when Colonel North undertook to be really a trifle severe with me, I flared up and offered my resignation on the spot. I told him that, if an officer couldn't leave post for a little fun, without the hanged formality of reporting and securing permission, then the Army was no place for a gentleman."

"Did Colonel North let you get away with that?" demanded Lieutenant Johnson.

"He did," confessed Algy, "for in his good old soldierly heart he knew that I hadn't arrived at the dignity even of being a dub. Then I wired my father and asked him to see the President and get my resignation through at once. Instead, my father wired that he'd had me ordered to the Service Schools at Fort Leavenworth; that I'd have to go there, work like blazes and make good, or else

36

that he'd disown me and make me work for a living. I thought the Service Schools would be easier than working for a living," added Algy reminiscently, "but from what I went through at Leavenworth I'd advise any lazy man to go to work instead."

"It's tough at Leavenworth," assented Brisbane. "I put in a year there once."

"I'm glad, now, that I went to Leavenworth," Algy continued. "I was taught there that a soldier's life is about the finest going, if only a fellow can buckle down to work and discipline, and forget that he has any preferences of his own for anything."

"Leavenworth certainly made a good soldier of you, Ferrers," put in Sears. "I don't know a harder-working officer than you are to-day."

"Thank you," came from Algy. "But that seems hard for you to believe, doesn't it, Overton?"

"From the past, Ferrers, yes; but not from what I see of you now, or from what I heard you saying as you came into the club."

"Why, Ferrers is called one of the worst grinds in the service," laughed Lieutenant Hapgood. "Overton, I know it to be a fact that Algy Ferrers, for the last year, has been returning all the remittances that his father sent him. Algy simply wrote back that, by the time he had his day's work done, he was too tired to go out and spend money."

"Well, why not?" challenged Algy. "A second lieutenant is paid seventeen hundred dollars a year. To my way of thinking that's all an honest, hard-working young fellow ought to be allowed to have."

"You can't keep many automobiles on that," smiled Noll.

"I don't have to," retorted Algy. "I haven't been in an auto, except under orders, since I left Clowdry for Leavenworth."

A wonderful change had come about in the case of Algy Ferrers. Hal and Noll felt like pinching themselves to see if they would wake up.

"Every younger officer, nowadays, has to put in two or three spells of study at the Service Schools," continued Algy, turning to the two newest members of the club. "It does 'em a lot of good, too. You'll run up against it one of these days, without a doubt. If you've any angles the Service School will rub 'em off. They try to be kind to you at Leavenworth, Terry. One of their plans, there, is to give you time for eight hours' sleep, but you can't always connect. All the rest of the time is working day. Why, I've gone to my quarters at Leavenworth so tired out at night that I've sat down in a chair for a moment, to try to rest a bit before undressing. Then my eyes would close, and the next thing I'd know it would be daylight—and I'd slept all night in my chair with my clothes on. That's no fanciful picture either." Algy finished plaintively. "A married man is in huge luck at Leavenworth, if he has a good wife."

"Why?" Noll wanted to know.

"Because the poor student officer can usually depend upon his wife to wake him in time to shave before the next day's grind begins. You will know all about it when your turn comes to be detailed at Leavenworth."

By this time the meal was over. Some of the officers had begun to smoke, those who did not use tobacco, lingered over their coffee.

Lieutenant Pratt drew a pasteboard box from an inside pocket, took from it a cigarette, lighted it and lay the box beside his plate.

"You might be good," put in Hapgood, "and pass me a cigarette."

"Had I known that you wanted one, Hapgood, you'd have had this one," explained Lieutenant Pratt apologetically. "It was the last one in the box."

"I don't see that I smoke, then, as there's no waiter in the room," sighed Hapgood, with an air of comic discontent.

"Try Ferrers," advised Hal. "He never moves anywhere with less than a hundred cigarettes about him."

"I?" demanded Algy, wheeling, a flush mounting to his cheeks and temples. "Not guilty, I'm glad to say."

"Why, you used——" began Hal.

"All bygones," declared Algy. "I know I used to walk around looking like an empty house on fire, but Leavenworth changed that, too. The second day I was there I lighted a coffin-nail before one of the older officers. Wish you could have seen him go for me! It was all smooth as velvet, and eloquent of courtesy, but that old officer said——"

Algy halted suddenly in his speech.

"*What?*" chorused half a dozen others.

"I'm not going to tell you," Ferrers made answer. "There are too many smokers here, and I don't intend to make any enemies out of good fellows."

"Tell us, do," coaxed Pratt. "We don't hold you responsible, Ferrers. We'll charge the jolt up to the old officer you mentioned."

"Well, then," resumed Algy, "he asked me what I meant by making a foul chimney of my nose and stewing my brain all day long in a mess of nicotine. He further asked me why I didn't give it up."

"What did you say to him?"

"Why," confessed Algy honestly, "I told him that it had never occurred to me before that a cigarette smoker is violating the nuisance act all day long, and that an Army officer could be in better business than breaking the minor laws."

"Thank you," said Pratt dryly, rising and walking over to a fire place, into which he threw his lighted cigarette. A general laugh greeted the act.

"You two used to be clean young fellows, with no cigarettes in your pockets," continued Ferrers, turning to Hal and Noll.

"We don't smoke yet," answered Terry.

Brisbane, the ranking officer present, arose, and the others followed.

"Now, Overton, it's ten minutes to two," explained Lieutenant Sears, glancing at his watch. "If you want to go over to Captain Foster's quarters, and be presented to him, I'm at your service."

"Thank you; I'm ready."

At the same time Lieutenant Johnson made the same offer to Noll. The four officers left the club together, all returning the salutes of a sentry who stood at present arms.

"What's all that nonsense Ferrers gives us about the old days when he was such a rookie from civil life?" inquired Lieutenant Sears.

"It's all true enough," Hal answered. "Ferrers was a mighty good-hearted fellow——"

"He is now," interposed Sears.

"But he was really the laughing-stock of all the enlisted men, and the despair of all the other officers at Fort Clowdry," continued Hal. "Nothing has pleased me so much, in a long time, as to see him such a dead-in-earnest, dyed-in-the-wool officer as he is now."

"Ferrers is one of the most capable youngsters in the service," Sears declared warmly. "Really, you know, it seems incredible that he could ever have been any other kind of officer."

"If a man like Algy Ferrers can come back, and be what he is to-day," Noll declared, "then there's hope for a pair of raw youngsters like Overton and myself."

"Oh, you two will have no trouble; you've been enlisted men," replied Johnson. "Men who come up from the ranks, as you two did, have had all the possible nonsense knocked out of them before they got to their first examinations. But here's Captain Goodale's house."

"And Captain Foster's is the next beyond," stated Lieutenant Sears.

CHAPTER IX

ORDERED TO FRONTIER DUTY

"YOU'VE all your equipment with you, Mr. Overton?" inquired Captain Foster, of H company, after the presentation had been made and Lieutenant Sears had withdrawn.

"Yes, sir."

"You'll want much of your time to-day for getting to rights in your quarters, Mr. Overton. You'll be required only to turn out for parade at the end of the afternoon. To-morrow you will enter fully upon your duties. Mr. Sears will post you thoroughly at mess this evening."

"Very good, sir."

"That is all I have in the way of instructions. Wait, and I'll see if I can find Mrs. Foster. I want you to meet her."

A few moments later Hal found himself chatting with Mrs. Foster, a very sweet little woman, some years younger than the captain. Hal took an instant liking to her. Mrs. Foster asked him much about his home folks, adding:

"As soon as you feel that you're settled in your new life and duties, Mr. Overton, I shall ask you to permit me to invite your mother here as my guest. I know that a mother always wants to see her son's life in the service."

"When that time comes, Mrs. Foster," the young officer answered, "you will be giving me the greatest happiness that can come to me."

"Well," pursued that good lady, "it will not take you so very long to get settled in your new duties. The time for your mother's visit need not be so very far away."

"You forget one thing, my dear," interposed the captain.

"And what is that?" questioned Mrs. Foster.

"You forget the Mexican rebels."

"Those barefooted, half-starved ragamuffins!" cried Mrs. Foster. "*They* can have nothing to do with our plans here at the post."

"On the contrary, they may be mischievous enough to upset the whole routine of garrison life. You have read something about the Mexican rebels, Mr. Overton?"

"I have seen a few paragraphs in the newspaper, sir," Hal answered. "Enough to know that some pretender in the country across the border is trying to upset the present government in his own interests."

"What do you think, Overton, about the chances of that rebellion?"

"As far, sir, as I have been able to form any opinion from the press accounts, it seems that only a few hundred of the rebels are in the field, and that they are spending most of their time in running away from the troops of the Mexican government."

"Ah, but the fact that the rebels are in the field, instead of in their graves, shows that their movement possesses some stability," replied Captain Foster. "The fact is that other Mexicans over here on the Texas side are organizing to go to the aid of the rebels just across the Rio Grande. Our government has information that the Mexican sympathizers in this state have secured a good many stands of rifles and a considerable supply of ammunition, and are watching their chance to slip over the border into Mexico with their war supplies. Now, the few hundred rebels at present in the field in Mexico may be joined by enough more Mexicans from this side to make an army of two or three thousand men. If so many get together under the standard of the rebel leader, then more thousands will flock in answer to the call. The rebel army may be ten thousand strong next week, and twenty thousand the week after."

"But surely," interposed Mrs. Foster, "this government will not allow the Mexican rebels on this side of the river to take their war supplies across the river into Mexico?"

"Not if our government can stop the operation," smiled Captain Foster. "But, my dear, how would the government stop it?"

"By the use of the troops, I suppose," replied Mrs. Foster.

"Exactly. And did you know that Wilshire's and Apthorpe's troops of cavalry have been ordered to patrol the border in small riding parties, for the very purpose of stopping such expeditions into Mexico?"

"No!"

"Nor did I, until Major Tipton informed me, only a little while ago. Further, Tipton has been directed to hold the troops at this post ready for work in patroling the frontier. That was why I just suggested that Mr. Overton will do well to wait until this border business has blown over before he encourages you to invite his mother. Mrs. Overton might arrive here only to find her son absent on several weeks of hard hiking."

"Am I discreet in asking you, Captain, whether you think it likely that this battalion will be called out for frontier patrol duty?" asked Lieutenant Hal.

"I think it highly likely that at least three-fourths of this command will soon be called out on such duty," replied the captain of H company.

Hal's eyes gleamed.

"You seem to like the prospect, my boy."

"I do, sir. Active service always appeals to me."

"You'll find it very active service," sniffed Mrs. Foster. "Nothing but a lot of hard, dusty marching, with insufficient food, little time to prepare it, and always matching wits with a lot of crafty, barefooted Mexicans!"

"Overton is right," contended the captain. "Despite the discomforts and possible hardships such work is excellent, both for soldiers and their officers."

"If anything of the sort comes," murmured Lieutenant Hal, "I certainly hope that I shan't be left out of it."

"You probably won't," replied Captain Foster dryly. "Major Tipton has been informed that both Mr. Terry and yourself have already distinguished yourselves in scouting work in the field. You will have use for such talents here, if we are called out to watch the border."

"It's stupid work," cried Mrs. Foster petulantly, "and it will spoil several of the good times that the ladies at this post have been planning."

"Now, we won't detain Mr. Overton any longer, my dear," remarked the captain. "Remember, Overton, parade this afternoon. No other duties for to-day."

Hal took his leave, returning, light-footed, to bachelor quarters. There he found Noll, returned before him.

"Nothing but parade for me to-day, Noll," Hal called to his chum.

"Same here," rejoined young Terry, opening his door. "May I come across into your house a little while?"

"I shall be glad to have you if you have no more to do than I appear to have. My striker appears to have put everything in apple-pie order. Sit down. How do you like the new station and the crowd?"

"Fine," nodded Noll. "Major Tipton appears to be just the right sort of commanding officer."

The instant that the first call for parade sounded Lieutenants Hal and Noll sprang from their chairs. Both were soon going down the stairs, their swords clanking at their sides. This parade, though unimportant in a sense, was their first actual duty as line officers. Both youngsters walked with a new dignity and erectness as they crossed to the parade ground.

They were the first officers to appear. When the actual parade call sounded the enlisted men of four companies came out in human streams from the barracks buildings.

Now the remaining officers of the garrison came briskly up while the first sergeants of the companies were attending to the formation.

At the proper moment the officers of the battalion went to their stations. As he drew his sword, for the first time in Uncle Sam's service, Lieutenant Hal felt a thrill the like of which he had never known before.

Neither youngster made a mistake during the maneuvers and ceremonies of parade. Though it was the first time that either had stood with troops as officers,

41

they went through all the movements mechanically. They had not put in three years in the ranks for nothing.

Yet every moment, every movement of parade now had a new significance to the young lieutenants. Then, when it was all over, and the men dismissed, the officers returned to their quarters to prepare for dinner.

Hal and Noll reached mess ten minutes ahead of the dinner hour. Most of the officers who would dine at the club were already present.

"Mr. Sears," asked Hal, going over to his first lieutenant, "can you spare me a little time after dinner?"

"Easily, Overton. You want to ask me about the routine duties, I imagine."

"Yes. Captain Foster has ordered me to full duty beginning with to-morrow."

"Then we'll find seats in the reading room after dinner. It won't take very long to give you the schedule and the inside ropes."

In the Army punctuality is made a prime virtue for both officers and men. Hence there were no laggards at dinner. Every officer took his seat at the long table at the minute of 6.30. Hapgood, who was officer of the day, came in with his sword at his side; he placed that weapon in a handy corner.

"The evening's news is that the Thirty-fourth is back in Colorado," announced Lieutenant Brisbane, glancing down the table.

"Just before we started west we read that their transport had arrived at San Francisco," answered Noll.

"And Major Silsbee's first battalion is at its old station, Fort Clowdry," added Mr. Brisbane. "By way of further news I may add that Major Tipton told me, a few minutes ago, that Major Silsbee had been ordered by wire to hold his battalion in readiness for a call from this department."

"Mexican border troubles?" asked Lieutenant Hapgood.

"Yes."

"Then the government knows, better than we do, that the border trouble threatens to grow acute," remarked Lieutenant Sears. "It has been understood, I think, that troops from this post will be the first infantry ordered out to the support of the two cavalry troops now patroling."

"Oh, we'll get some of that barefoot business presently," grumbled Pratt. "A beastly job. The state of Texas ought to call out its police to take care of the matter."

"Except," remarked Sears dryly, "that it is the province of the United States, not of a single state, to preserve neutrality at the border."

"It's cases like this Mexican business that make a fellow wish that he belonged to the Navy," insisted Pratt. "If we go out, as doughboys, we'll have to tramp and hike until our shoes are full of sore feet, and all for nothing, perhaps. If we belonged to the Navy, and were ordered to patrol, we'd do it in a gunboat, and wouldn't care where we went, as we'd always be on our gunboat, with, good meals ready at the stroke of the bell, with baths, clean clothing, even easy chairs right at hand. The Navy can keep on patroling even while two-thirds of a crew are in their berths enjoying sweet sleep until the moment for action comes."

"Stop it," insisted Algy Ferrers. "Even in the Navy you'd find you'd have to work like a horse. There are no easy ways of getting through life, and a soldier ought not to look for 'em."

Pratt, who was a husky and sufficiently energetic young officer at need, and who had merely been exercising his right to grumble, flushed and was silent.

"I don't suppose Terry or myself will have the luck to be picked for this sort of border patrol work, if it comes," suggested Hal.

"Probably you'll be kept on post until you're more accustomed to your men," nodded Lieutenant Hapgood.

"Either way will suit me," said Noll. "I don't expect to have my pick of anything until I've served a few years more."

"You won't have it then either," laughed Sears.

The meal over, Sears retired into a corner with Hal. Johnson joined them with Noll. The two youngest officers in the regiment were handed printed slips containing the routine work of the day at Fort Butler, and also the hour for the call to each duty. Sears and Johnson added much more information.

"You'll come to us for anything else that you want to know, of course," said Sears, in conclusion. "You are aware, of course, that your superior officers are paid to answer questions."

"Thank you," acknowledged Hal.

It was soon nine o'clock, and the two Army boys, tired with their day of travel and of new life, left the club early, going directly to quarters and to Hal's room.

"I won't stay long," declared Noll, sinking into the easy chair that his chum pushed forward. "But I've simply got to talk a bit with you, bunkie, my head is so full of it all."

The chums chatted on until at last the notes of a bugle were borne to their ears.

"Listen!" cried Hal, holding up one hand, his eyes glowing. "The same good old Army taps!"

"We don't have to go to bed, since we added swords to our equipment," laughed Noll.

"No; but we had better turn in. We have as much work to do as any of the enlisted men."

An hour later, when all was quiet, there came a heavy pounding on Hal's door. As the young lieutenant awoke and leaped from his bed he was sure that he heard a similar commotion going on at Noll's door.

"Who is it?" called Hal, throwing on a bathrobe and going toward the hall door.

"Private Graham, of the guard, sir. Major Tipton's compliments to Lieutenant Overton, and the major directs that the lieutenant report immediately at headquarters."

Then, as Hal and Noll both opened their doors, the soldier added:

"Major Tipton authorized me to add, sir, that the Mexican border trouble has broken out, and that you'll both march soon with your men."

CHAPTER X

ON THE SCENE OF BORDER TROUBLE

THE speed with which a soldier can dress, and do it tidily, would astonish the average civilian.

Very soon after the call had sounded at their doors Hal and Noll, their swords hanging at their left sides and their revolvers belted on, stepped in at headquarters.

"Come right in, gentlemen," called Major Tipton, from the rear office.

Lieutenant Brandon, battalion adjutant, was already with his chief.

"Your first call has come sooner than you expected," smiled Major Tipton. "Captain Foster will be here presently, and then we will go over the matter together. Ah, Foster! Come right in."

Then the orders were made clear.

"The department commander has directed me to send one company, or its equivalent, up to the village of Agua Dulce," stated the major. "You know where the village is, Captain—about twenty miles up the river. You will start within the hour. Now, for the sake of giving our youngest officers practice in handling their men I am going to send the second platoons of F and H companies, and you, Foster, will command. You will take one wall tent for the officers, Captain, and the men will each carry their half of a shelter tent. You will take kitchen kit for one company, and fifty rounds of ammunition for each man—though I trust you will have no occasion to fire any shots. The quartermaster is now ordering out three escort wagons to accompany you. If your provisions run low you will receive more. You should be in camp, Captain, soon after daylight."

"Agua Dulce," continued Major Tipton, "as you know, is a village with a large proportion of Mexican population. The War Department is advised that the Mexican rebels are making the village an American headquarters for the insurrection. It will be your duty, Captain, to see that no armed parties or cargoes of munitions of war get across the river. You will very likely find that Mexican troops are stationed on the opposite side of the river. If you so find, you will act in harmony, as far as you can, with the commander of the Mexican troops."

"Very good, Major."

"I have already sent the guard to notify the first sergeants of F and H companies to turn out the second platoons of each company. You now have your orders in full, Captain."

"Very good, sir."

The three officers saluted their commander and withdrew. No word was spoken as the three crossed the parade ground, going toward barracks.

Outside a lot of soldiers had already appeared, many of them looking decidedly drowsy. But there were no complaints. "Kickers" are never popular in the Army.

"Ranking sergeants of each platoon report here," called Captain Foster quietly, as he halted. "You will be prepared for assembly and roll call within forty-five minutes. Immediately afterwards the command will march. Any further orders you will take from your respective platoon commanders."

With a nod to Hal and Noll, Captain Foster strode away toward the quartermaster stables, to see how near ready the escort wagons and their loads might be.

"Keep the two platoons apart," ordered Hal, going over to the men. "We want to know which platoon is ready for duty first. Sergeant Raney, go back into barracks and see what is detaining the absentees."

"Sergeant Klein, you will also look up your missing ones," directed Noll.

Both non-coms and men worked faster after that. Hal and Noll had served long enough in the ranks to know that some drowsy men might remain behind as long as possible, dozing in some corner.

As soon as it was discovered that both lieutenants were keenly alert to their duties, greater speed was shown in assembling the men. Five minutes later all the soldiers had turned out, ready. Some of the men in Hal's platoon began to shoulder their blanket rolls.

"Leave your blanket rolls on the ground," directed Hal, stepping over to his men. "It is a warm night, and there's no need of carrying weight until you have to."

Captain Foster soon returned, having satisfied himself that work with the escort wagons was progressing rapidly.

"All the men of my platoon are out, sir, and ready to move," Hal reported, saluting.

"All my men ready, too, sir," Noll added.

"Quick work," nodded Captain Foster. "The escort wagons will be here within fifteen minutes. We shall be able to make an earlier start than ordered."

A few minutes later three escort wagons, each well laden and hauled by a team of mules, came out on to the road.

"Let your men fall in. Hold separate roll calls. Report as soon as ready," directed Captain Foster.

The two platoons, drawn up in one rank with a slight interval between, were soon in readiness.

"March your platoons," called Captain Foster.

"F company, fours left, march," ordered Noll.

"H company, fours left, march," followed Hal.

Off into the night moved a compact column of men in fours, a sergeant at the head of each platoon, and the two lieutenants on the flanks. Captain Foster noted the start with approval. The column moved on down the road, past the escort wagons, which then fell in at the rear.

"Give the men the route step, now," murmured Captain Foster, going past Hal up to the head of the line.

"Route step, march," ordered Lieutenant Hal. In another moment the men of the leading platoon had also fallen into the route step.

"We'll march four miles to the first halt," said Captain Foster, falling in beside Noll.

The road turned to the right, heading west. When the first halt was called the column stopped on a lonely stretch of the highway, in sight of the Rio Grande. After ten minutes the column started again. There were frequent halts, after that, but soon after daylight had come the column made its last halt just outside the village of Agua Dulce.

Now camp was quickly made. A soldier, no matter how fatigued, is never too tired to eat. Several score of little fagot fires were soon blazing briskly, and over these coffee was made and bacon fried. The next meal would be furnished by the company cook. Within half an hour after pitching tents breakfast had been eaten, and much progress made with unpacking the escort wagons.

"Mr. Terry, you will remain in command of the camp. Keep ten men awake for duty, and relieve the men in two hours. Let the men not on duty sleep. Mr. Overton, you will accompany me into the village."

A ten minutes' walk brought Captain Foster and Hal into Agua Dulce. It was an insignificant little village, of perhaps eight hundred inhabitants. Five hundred of these were Mexicans. There are many such towns on the Texas border. The Mexicans were engaged somewhat in trade, but most of them belonged to the floating class. They were cowboys, sheep-herders and laborers. Few of them represented a high grade of Mexican citizenship. Many were "wanted" in Mexico for minor offenses, for which the extradition treaty did not provide. Living only from day to day, usually from hand to mouth, and nearly always discontented, this sort of Mexican was excellent material out of which to make a revolutionist.

"It doesn't look like much of a place for a headquarters against the powerful Mexican government," Captain Foster confided to his young lieutenant. "Yet it is in just such places as this that a successful revolution in Mexico may some day start. It might happen in this year as well as in any other. A few thousand rifles and enough cartridges could be shipped from this point, across the river, on a dark night. With this happening at several such points enough munitions for an Army might be ferried across. With men waiting on the other side a rebel army could be easily started."

"It seems a pity, doesn't it, sir, for us to have to interfere in such matters?" asked Lieutenant Hal.

"No; for the United States is on friendly terms with the government of Mexico. Therefore, under the laws of nations, we are obliged to see to it that all caution is used to prevent the shipment of arms to revolutionists on the other side of the river. Mexico would have to do as much for us if the case were reversed."

"But the case never is reversed," smiled Hal.

"It came near being, once. At the outset of the Spanish war, when there were a good many Spaniards living in Mexico, some of them started a foolish movement to organize and project an armed force of Spaniards over the border into Texas. The Spaniards had a notion that they could slip over the border, do a lot of harm and get safely back into Mexico. But the Mexican government sent out its secret service agents to run down the plot, and also sent two or three regiments of the Mexican army to patrol the border."

"What did the people of Texas think of that, sir?"

46

Captain Foster laughed.

"The Texans were really mad as hornets," he continued. "They said they wished the Mexican government would mind its own business and not spoil sport. The Texans were just aching to have a few thousand Spaniards come over the border and start things going. None of the Spaniards would ever have got back into Mexico; the Texans would have taken care of that. But here we are in the village, and now we'll have to start making inquiries."

This consumed two or three hours. The postmaster was seen, and then some of the other Texans. The railroad did not touch Agua Dulce, but there were two big trucking concerns that handled freight from the nearest railroad point. There were also several Mexican teamsters in the place; these latter could hardly be depended upon to give accurate information. The American teamsters all declared that they had handled no suspicious-looking freight for Mexicans.

"But you'll find a lot of long, shallow boxes stored in Pedro Guarez's stable, if what I've heard is right," added one of the truckmen.

"Look like rifle cases, do they?" inquired Captain Foster.

"That's what I judge from what I've heard. Mexican teamsters have been bringing in the cases for the last three nights."

"Where is the barn of this fellow, Guarez?"

"Come upstairs, Captain, and I can point it out to you from the roof. But don't let any of the Greasers know that I told you about this, for I have to be on the road many a dark night, and these Greasers are a bad lot, especially just now. And listen, Captain! Don't get so far into Guarez's barn that you couldn't get out handily. If you do you may never come out. The Greasers are especially ugly these last few days, and I don't believe it would take much to start 'em off."

CHAPTER XI

LIEUTENANT HAL'S SWORD GUARDS THE DOOR

HAVING learned the location of the barn, which was about a third of a mile away, Captain Foster signed to Lieutenant Hal to accompany him.

"I shall leave you outside of the barn when I go in, Mr. Overton. You may have a crowd around you in no time, for these Mexicans are easily excited. Be careful to handle them smoothly, and not to start any unnecessary trouble. At the same time, keep your eyes and ears wide open for any news that you may hear. Do you understand Spanish?"

"I know a little of the kind that I learned in the Philippines," Hal answered.

"You may be able to understand the Mexican patter, then. But don't let them know that you understand it."

A brisk walk brought the two Army officers to one of the most substantial houses in the Mexican quarter. It was a two-story frame house, kept in a fairly tidy condition. Behind the house was a wooden barn, still larger.

Captain Foster did not trouble himself to approach the house, around which there were no signs of life. Instead he walked hurriedly through the yard. Just as the two officers neared the barn the door was seen to slide on its roller.

"Keep them from closing that door, Overton!" cried Captain Foster. Hal bounded forward, thrusting his right foot in the crack just in time to prevent the door closing.

"I'll help you push that door open again," cried the captain. Between them they succeeded, driving the door back, wide open, revealing two scowling young Mexican hostlers.

"You g'way!" snarled one of them in a surly tone.

"Where's your master, Pedro Guarez?" demanded Captain Foster.

"Dunno. He far away. G'way. I wanta close this door."

"Don't you attempt to do it," warned Captain Foster stiffly. "Mr. Overton, stand here and see that these fellows don't close the door. I'm going to, look around inside."

Just as Captain Foster stepped into the barn a rear door of the house opened quickly. A Mexican, rather better dressed than the average, ran hastily across the yard.

"Here," he cried, in good English, though he panted as he reached the barn, "you must leave. You have no right here!"

"Only Pedro Guarez can tell me that," retorted the captain.

"But I am Pedro Guarez."

"Then you're the man I want to see," returned Captain Foster, fixing Guarez with his keen eyes. "I am going to look through your barn and I may ask you a lot of questions."

"I shall not answer, if you do. Get out! You have no right here!"

"Then get a policeman, and get him here to arrest me," smiled the captain.

A murmuring of excited voices was heard out in the road, after which, half a dozen Mexicans came hurriedly into the yard. They quickly crowded around the door.

"You have a good many friends interested in your affairs, Mr. Guarez," insinuated the captain. "But come on; I am going through the barn."

"I cannot say that it will be safe," retorted Guarez, with an expressive shrug of his shoulders.

"Safe?" echoed Captain Foster sternly. "That's a question that an American soldier never asks."

"Just as you will, then, Señor Capitain," returned Guarez. "I protest, but I cannot fight you—alone."

"And you'd better stop all that talk of fighting, too," warned the captain. "Come, if you want to go through with me."

Just then about a score more of excited Mexicans poured into the yard.

"You see," cautioned Guarez. "You will stir up a lot of trouble, Señor Capitain."

"Mr. Overton, don't let any of the rabble come into this barn for the present," directed Hal's company commander. "Come, Guarez, if you wish."

The Mexican hesitated, for an instant. But he saw Captain Foster walk toward the haymow.

"Come on, my friends!" cried Guarez. "You, too, shall see what this too-officious soldier dares to do here!"

He spoke in Spanish, but Captain Foster understood, and so did Hal Overton. Instantly there was an excited rush on the part of the Mexican loungers outside, who tried to crowd past Hal.

"Back, all of you!" ordered the young lieutenant. He spoke in English, accompanying his order with a gesture that any man might understand.

But the Mexicans pressed against him, scowling and shaking their heads as though to imply that they did not understand.

"Get back, every one of you," insisted Lieutenant Hal. "You know well enough what I am telling you."

However, the Mexicans at the rear of the compact little crowd pushed against those in front. The Army boy was in danger of being pushed off his feet.

In an instant Hal's right hand flew to the hilt of his sword. He spoke no word, now, but his face was white, his lips set and stern. The gleam in his eyes boded no good to the men in front of him.

Swish! The sword leaped from its scabbard, its keen blade gleaming in the air as Lieutenant Hal made a swift cut about him. The steel struck no one, for the rabble drew back swiftly. Some thirty pairs of eyes flashed hatred at the Army boy.

"Now, *keep* your distance," warned the Army boy, coolly returning his sword to its scabbard.

"Surely we can draw some steel of our own, friends," muttered one of the Mexicans. "If this soldier boy resists us again, or places his hand to his sword, let every man among us draw his own steel and rush in over his body!"

Hal heard and comprehended, perfectly, but his orders had been not to let the Mexicans see that he understood their talk. So he stood there, smiling coolly.

"Peace, friends, for a moment," broke in another Mexican, speaking in Spanish. "Then, if this young *soldado* does not yield, it will be time to rush over him. If we finish him, no one can afterwards swear whose knife did the deed. After that the same thrust for his captain."

Again Hal Overton comprehended, but he glanced, in cool inquiry, at the speaker as that fellow stepped forward.

"See here, soldier," began the Mexican, speaking fluently in English, "Don Pedro has invited us into this barn. You have no lawful right to stop us."

"I won't argue that with you," the young lieutenant answered steadily.

"But you will have to let us pass. We are going inside. So why should you take a lot of blows that you need not receive? And my countrymen are excitable, some of them. I do not know that one or two of them could be restrained from using a knife on you."

"They'll know more afterward, if they try it," laughed Hal, as though the situation amused him. "But I would advise your friends not to try it. You and they are going to move back, now, and thereafter any man who gets within ten feet of me I am going to run through with my sword."

Hal tapped the hilt of his weapon lightly, then started to push the rabble back. There were many mutterings. Lieutenant Overton did not know at what instant he might feel the sharp prick of steel. If he felt any fear of such a fate nothing in his cool smile betrayed him. The crowd fell back, though there was no assurance

49

that their smouldering wrath might not flame up at any moment. Hal's life still hung on a thread. A breath, and these sullen, excitable men would hurl themselves upon him.

In the meantime, Guarez, realizing that his friends might not come immediately to his assistance, had scowlingly followed Captain Foster to the haymow. That officer picked up a pitchfork and began to prod the hay.

"I forbid this!" cried Guarez, in a deep, dramatic voice. Captain Foster paid no heed. Soon the captain drove his implement through the hay, and against something that gave back a resistance like that of soft pine. With a skill that he had acquired as a boy on a farm the captain began to pitch the hay.

"Stop! You have no right!" thundered the Mexican. But Captain Foster had uncovered two packing cases and continued energetically with his work.

"Will you stop?" howled the Mexican, advancing upon the man in uniform.

"No," returned Foster briefly. "I'm here on business."

"Come in, my friends!" howled Pedro Guarez. "Never mind the young tailor's model at the door."

The Mexicans outside heard, and the appeal frenzied them. Four or five started toward the barn-door, the rest closing in behind them.

Swish! Lieutenant Hal's sword was again in the air.

"Who wants to come first?" demanded the Army boy dryly.

The rabble paused, then crowded back slowly. There was something in Hal Overton's cold, steady, masterful eyes that awed them more than any fears of their own.

Captain Foster tossed and threw hay with a will until he had uncovered a compact pile of small packing cases.

"Sixty," he announced, after a quick estimation. "And each case, Guarez, contains ten rifles. Six hundred in all—enough with which to equip quite a respectable *insurrecto* regiment on the other side of the Rio Grande."

"There are no rifles there, nothing with which to make war," snarled the fellow.

"I accept your statement, with reservations," replied Foster dryly.

"Even though they were rifles, the United States law does not forbid one to buy or sell guns," insisted the Mexican.

"No; but it does forbid your shipping them over the border," rejoined the captain.

"But I have not attempted to ship anything over the border."

"Nor will you, Guarez. I might continue my search, and unearth other rifles, or perhaps cartridges. But I know enough for my purpose, and I am through here."

Captain Foster turned and left the mow, followed by the owner of the place.

"Come, Mr. Overton," ordered the company commander, stepping to the side of his junior officer. The assembled Mexicans followed them with flashing eyes.

Out in the street Captain Foster espied an American cowboy in the near distance. Shouting, the captain attracted the attention of the man, who galloped up.

"Do you know where my men are encamped?" inquired Foster.

"Sure," nodded the cowboy.

"Will you do me the very great favor of taking a note to the officer in command at the camp?"

"Sure," nodded the cowboy, with the same brevity.

Captain Foster hastily wrote the note, handing it to the man in saddle.

"This talk-talk paper will be at your camp in less'n five minutes," volunteered the horseman. "You going to remain here. Captain, for a little while?"

"Yes."

"Then look out, or some of the Greasers will play jack-knife with you. They're just aching for trouble, Cap."

The cowboy was gone in a cloud of dust. Captain Foster and his lieutenant did not again attempt to enter Guarez's yard, but the older officer whispered something that made the younger officer smile.

Some twenty minutes later Sergeant Raney, of Hal's platoon, turned the nearest corner and marched down the street at the head of a file of twelve soldiers.

"Sergeant," announced Captain Foster, "there are at least six hundred rifles in that barn. I have no legal right to seize the guns while they lie there. You will camp here and mount guard."

"If any attempt is made to move the cases you will send men with them to make sure that they do not go to the river. If any attempt be made to send the cases away in small lots, so as to split your detachment, you will then signal the camp with the rockets that you have brought with you."

"Very good, sir."

"Pitch camp at once, and maintain watch over that barn day and night."

"Very good, sir."

An ominous growl ascended from the Mexicans, who had overheard. But, with a quiet smile at his lieutenant, Captain Foster walked away, remarking:

"They have guns enough there, Mr. Overton, but we've spiked 'em."

"But I suppose, sir, that the Mexicans may have other rifles at other points not so far from here."

"That we shall learn, Mr. Overton, as soon as we can. We shall also watch the river."

Captain Foster and his lieutenant then returned to camp for a brief period of rest. Both were well satisfied with the early forenoon's work.

There was, however, as Foster guessed, other and grimmer work yet ahead of the military.

CHAPTER XII

THE STEP OF THE STEALTHY ONE

BY noon the soldiers at camp found themselves well rested. Nearly all of them had had some hours of sleep.

The midday dinner was served, the officers eating at the same time, though sitting apart from their men. As they finished, Captain Foster said:

"Overton, I shall leave you in command of the camp this afternoon. I shall take Terry with me on a tramp through some of this surrounding country. I want to locate other contraband guns or cartridges, if I can. Except for necessary duties let the men rest. While we are on this duty most of the work will be done at night. Sleep a part of the afternoon yourself; one of the non-commissioned officers can look after the camp, and call you at need."

His sole sleep lately having been for an hour the night before, Lieutenant Hal needed no urging to seek a cot in the wall-tent set apart for the use of the officers.

"When will you sleep, sir?" Noll ventured to ask.

"When I have time," replied Captain Foster, stifling a yawn and smiling. "This will not be the first time that I have worked for forty hours without sleep."

But the afternoon prowl revealed no more rifles. There was another surprise. At Agua Dulce were fourteen boats belonging to private owners—all the craft at the village water front. Five of the boats were owned by Mexicans. Somewhat disappointed, Captain Foster and Lieutenant Noll returned to camp.

At the evening meal, just before dark, Captain Foster remarked:

"I've posted a corporal and a guard to see that none of the boats leave shore until they've been found to contain no freight that looks like munitions of war. To my surprise none of the Mexicans showed the slightest interest in my doings. It begins to look as though they have no intention of trying to ferry arms over the frontier at present."

"Are there any steam craft at this point, sir?" inquired Lieutenant Hal.

"Nothing of the sort, Mr. Overton."

"Then, if the Mexicans do plan to get any war supplies over the frontier, don't you imagine that they have arranged for a launch or a tug to drop down the river, or come up the stream, from some other point?"

"That's worth thinking of," muttered the captain, looking thoughtful.

"A boat engaged in such secret work would probably also take the risk of running without lights."

"But a steamer would be bound to make noise enough to give us warning when she attempted to come in toward the shore," pursued Captain Foster.

"That, sir, will depend on how far apart our guards are to-night, or on such other night as the Mexicans may make the attempt."

"Now that our troops are here they may make no attempt," hinted Noll.

"They will if they dare," replied Captain Foster. "If there are six hundred rifles in Guarez's barn, and more elsewhere, then there must be a lot of Mexicans on the other side waiting impatiently for the supplies to reach them. Your suggestion, Mr. Overton, about a steamer, is one that must be kept in mind."

After some thought Captain Foster wrote a telegram, entrusting it to a corporal to take over to the village.

Hal was then directed to take sixty men and to dispose of them in suitable spots along the water-front. Fifty men were to be used for this purpose. A corporal and three men would then patrol along the easterly end of the line, Hal and the few remaining men of his command patroling the western end of the line. Either patrol would be quick to respond to any shot from a sentry.

"This is an exceedingly responsible task, Mr. Overton," Captain Foster informed the young officer. "If you fail at some point, then arms enough to equip a brigade of Mexican rebels may cross the river to-night."

"I shall keep every sense on the alert, sir."

Noll was given command of the camp. Captain Foster, now thoroughly fagged, turned in for a few hours' sleep, after leaving orders to be called at eleven o'clock.

"You will find me prowling about your lines from midnight on, Mr. Overton," was the captain's last word before turning in. "It is now nearly dark, so I suggest that you march your men without any unnecessary delay."

Two minutes later Lieutenant Hal was marching his command from camp. He did not take his column through the village. Instead, he marched it to the eastward, then over to the river bank.

Posting his fifty sentries about three hundred feet apart the Army boy thus covered a stretch of water-front some three miles in length, the village's strip of river front being nearly at the middle of this line. Corporal Smith's patrol was at the westerly end of the line. Hal himself headed the patrol at that end. The sentries were instructed to conceal themselves, in order to catch, if possible, any band of rebel smugglers in the act of loading war munitions on a craft.

"Nothing will come of it to-night," muttered Hal to himself, after he had placed his men. "The Mexicans here know that there are troops on the spot. If they were going to ship guns to-night they'd be sure to do it at some point ten or twenty miles from here. This is a job for a whole brigade of infantry. A regiment of cavalry could do more than three regiments of infantry on this work."

But Hal knew that the only two troops of cavalry so far ordered to frontier patrol were two troops at least a hundred miles to the westward. As yet Uncle Sam's soldiers were posted only at particular points known to harbor resolute Mexican rebels.

"The fish can get through the net without the least trouble," thought the young officer.

It was still, dark and quiet out here on the river front. There were no lights, and seemingly none astir except the soldiers.

"Corporal, you stay with the patrol. I'm going to do a little exploring on my own account," said Lieutenant Hal, after another hour had passed.

"Very good, sir," replied Corporal Dent.

Hal had no very definite objective when he started off eastward by himself. He had left his sword behind in camp, but his revolver rested in its holster on his right hip.

The more Lieutenant Hal thought about it the less he was inclined to feel that there was any likelihood that Mexicans would attempt to-night to cross the river anywhere in the neighborhood of United States troops.

"The leaders among these fellows all know that they're being watched," thought Hal, "and they won't take chances when success means so much to them. Now that the troops have come Guarez and his associates will take time to think this matter over. None the less I shall have to be as vigilant as though I knew that they meant business to-night. It would be a fearful black eye on my record as an officer, right at the start, if I allowed the Guarez crowd to get anything real over the river to-night."

As he strolled along the water front the young lieutenant passed one of his sentries every few hundred feet. Part of the Army boy's purpose in going along by himself was to make sure that each and all of his men were alert. Their vigil would last until daylight.

In course of time the young officer passed the public pier, standing empty and deserted at the foot of the street leading from the village down to the water front. There were several row-boats tied up here at one side. During the day-time they had been under other guard, but now they lay unwatched—to the casual eye. However, within short distances of the pier on either side the young lieutenant knew that he had sentries hidden.

Neither sentry communicated with Lieutenant Overton as he passed.

"They're wise men not to hail me here," thought the young lieutenant. "They can see who I am, and, if there are any Mexicans prowling about here in the shadows, the sentries will not betray themselves."

Hal went on past the pier a little distance.

"The whole village seems asleep," he muttered, looking toward the town. "Yet, if we have blocked Guarez's little game I'll wager it will be late before he retires to-night. He'll be too mad to sleep."

Hal had halted in the shadow of two trees, growing close together. As he stood there, glancing about him, he was certain that he saw some one moving behind a growth of bushes a little way up the road.

"Halt! Who's there?" called the young Army officer, in a low voice, yet one that would carry.

There came no answer, but Hal was positive that he had seen some one moving.

"Answer, there!" he called sharply, running forward, "or stand where you are. I'm going to look you over."

Being a good sprinter young Overton was soon on the spot where he was sure that he had seen some one. But now there was no one in sight. There were other clumps of bushes near, and the prowler might easily have hidden.

"If you won't come out," called Lieutenant Hal, as he began to move quickly from clump to clump, "I'll rout you out!"

Then, of a sudden, just as Lieutenant Hal turned away from a growth of bushes, he heard a stealthy step at his rear. Like a flash he turned. As he did so, a rope was cast over his head, pinioning his arms to his sides. Before he could move or resist he felt himself jerked to the ground with considerable violence.

In another instant Hal would have been on his feet, contriving to get the noose loose or shifted in some way, and he would have been full of fight.

But the stealthy one, a man of good size and swarthy of feature, hurled himself upon the body of the trapped young Army officer. A low whistle followed, and Hal heard others moving.

Then he felt the prick of steel at his throat as the Mexican whispered:

"Quiet! Our cause is worth more than your life!"

CHAPTER XIII

ENOUGH TO MAKE A MEXICAN LAUGH

THOUGH Hal's captor spoke English, he was unquestionably Mexican. His eyes gleamed with an unholy fire. Young Overton had no doubt that he recognized the type—a man who believed that he was serving the holy cause of liberty in his own country, and who would think a *Gringo* life of little value if it interfered with the cause of the rebels across the river.

The sharp point of that knife pressed so insistently against Hal's neck that the Army boy realized he could not move before the weapon would be driven into his throat.

"This is where it's wiser to keep still," muttered the young lieutenant to himself. "My sentries will hear, anyway. They'll soon have this maniac subdued."

Instead of the sentries four other Mexicans came hurrying up. Nor did they seem afraid to come running down the open road. And one of these brown-skinned men was Pedro Guarez himself.

"Aha! You have the dashing young *Gringo!*" laughed Pedro harshly. "Bueno!" (Good.)

"Take him from me," begged the one who held the knife. "Bind him. We want no more trouble to-night."

Pedro and the three other new-comers threw themselves upon the young Army officer, rolling him over on his face and wrenching his arms behind him for tying.

"His Arms Pinioned To His Sides."

Yet as he was flopped over Hal had the use of his mouth for an instant. Regardless of what the consequences might be to him he yelled lustily:

"Sentry! Lieutenant Overton—*trouble*!"

Instead of being angry Pedro Guarez laughed harshly.

"*Gringo*, if you are not more careful we shall have to gag you!"

In record time the young lieutenant's arms were bound at elbow and wrist. Hal put up a sturdy fight. Had he been on his feet, and confronting only the fists of his assailants, he might have won. But on the ground, face downward, with his assailants piling over him, he had little chance to make trouble.

"He's all right, now," chuckled Guarez. "If he tries to make any more noise throw him to the ground and gag him. If he shows fight give him the steel."

Two of the Mexicans seized Lieutenant Hal by the arm on either side, while Guarez led the way into a stretch of forest.

They were soon at the end of their walk. Lieutenant Overton gave a gasp of dismay as his gaze fell upon the recumbent forms of six of his men, every one of them bound. Twenty feet beyond them lay a heap of six rifles and as many ammunition belts. Hal's eyes roved from face to face, his men grinning back sheepishly at him.

"All of our sentries for a thousand feet on either side of the pier!" gasped the young lieutenant, in deep humiliation.

Pedro Guarez, laughing harshly, said to Hal:

"Bah! You *Gringos* are no men to compete with the sons of Mexico! You are like children to us, who roam always by night, in preference to the light of day. And there is much Indian blood in Mexican veins. Now, if you are wise, no harm will come to you. But if you make a noise or show fight—*so!*"

Guarez made a significant gesture across his throat.

"How did you men come to be taken, Simms?" asked Hal, of the nearest soldier, after his captors had forced him to lie on the ground with his men.

"A Greaser crept up behind me, sir, and threw a noose that got tangled around my windpipe," replied Private Simms. "He did it so swiftly and quietly, too, that not even Bolton on the next post heard him."

"I heard nothing, sir," confirmed Private Bolton, "until I heard a roaring in my own ears just after I got the noose trick, and then a lot of other Greasers piled on me."

Again Guarez laughed, though he added with a snarl:

"You will do well to stop the use of that word, Greaser, fellow. Otherwise you will feel the weight of a boot in your face. So!"

Guarez swung his foot back as though intending to plant a vicious kick in Bolton's face.

"Have done with cowardice, Guarez!" ordered Lieutenant Hal sternly.

"Oh!" sneered the Mexican. "Me? I do as I please, and it would give me joy to kick your head off."

"I'd bide my time, and make you swallow your own foot in time, if you did," retorted Hal undauntedly.

"Be not too bold, my very young friend," warned Guarez, "or I shall deal with you at my leisure by taking you across into Mexico with me to-night."

"Try it!" dared Hal contemptuously.

For answer Guarez struck his boot lightly against Overton's lips. It was not a hard blow, nor did it cause any pain, but the meanness of the action brought the hot blood to Lieutenant Hal's face.

"I'll wait my own time to make you apologize humbly for that, you contemptible, cowardly Greaser!" broke impetuously from the Army boy's insulted lips.

An instant after the words were out Lieutenant Hal regretted the use of the word Greaser. That word, as a term of contempt for people of another country should not have been uttered by an officer of the Army.

"Bah!" retorted Guarez. "Some other time for you, my young jaguar."

As he went away Guarez signed to his companions, who followed him. There were now left as guards over the military prisoners two Mexicans. These were each armed with a forty-five Colt's revolver, and both appeared to be wholly alert.

"If any one among you calls for help," remarked one of the guards, "my orders are to reward you with steel."

Throwing back his coat the fellow displayed the hilt of a poniard.

"What's the use of shouting?" demanded Hal indifferently, "when my other guards are beyond reach of my voice?"

The Mexican laughed quietly, adding something in Spanish in an undertone to his companion.

"I hope you don't blame us, sir?" asked Private Simms.

"How can I censure any of you?" asked Hal bitterly, "when I was caught myself by the same easy trick?"

"Don't tell me, after this," muttered Private Simms, "that a Mexican is stupid and has no brains."

Conversation, though allowed in low tones by the two Mexican guards, soon died out among the soldiers, every one of whom felt secretly disgusted and ashamed of himself.

Twenty minutes, or more, passed before Hal, lying with one ear to the ground, heard the somewhat distant sound of moving horses. Soon after the roll of wheels came to him. Then, around a corner of the road, not far away, wagons turned and made toward the shore of the Rio Grande.

"Moving day with you fellows, is it?" demanded Hal of the guard who spoke English.

The fellow chuckled quietly.

"You've outwitted us, haven't you?" demanded the young lieutenant dryly. "You're moving munitions of war toward the river. You expect to ship them soon—but perhaps you won't succeed."

"You may prevent, if you can," laughed the Mexican.

"We shall see what will happen," retorted the Army boy.

"Nothing—so far as you American soldiers are concerned," came the triumphant answer.

"You shall see," vaunted Hal, though inwardly he groaned. He had been outwitted, in his first command as an officer, and he could feel the hot shame of the whole thing.

"But I don't see how you fellows can get anything out of Guarez's barn, unless you have been able to noose the whole of the sergeant's guard posted there."

Another laugh, and one of undisguised, unmistakable merriment, escaped the Mexican.

"Eh?" wondered Hal, for that laugh set him to thinking. Yet he did not pretend to himself that he could fathom what lay behind that laugh.

"It is our night to laugh," explained the guard.

"Your merriment is ill-timed, then," growled young Overton. "Wait until you have all your war stuff on Mexican soil before you laugh again!"

"My time to laugh is every time that I look at you seven brave *soldados*, tied up like so many chickens for the butcher," grinned the guard. "In the meantime, our boat must now be at the pier, and soon she will be laden. Then—ah, well, there will be rejoicing on the other side of the Rio Grande!"

"I'll wager there'll be rejoicing," thought Lieutenant Hal. "And, as for me, I'm an officer with a blasted reputation. I've failed with my first chance to do my duty!"

In sheer disgust with himself, though he was really little if any at fault, Lieutenant Hal Overton, U. S. Army, rolled further over that he might cool his hot face against the cool earth.

CHAPTER XIV

AFFAIRS TAKE A MILITARY TURN

AS he did so Hal's hands touched against the wrists of Private Simms, who lay next to him.

"Confound me, why didn't I think of that before?" the Army boy demanded of himself, a sudden, brief hope surging up in his breast.

Then he tried it, to see how well it would work.

Though he was bound at elbows and wrists, the young lieutenant's fingers were free. Wriggling slightly nearer, Hal fingered at the cords that bound Simm's wrists. That soldier felt and understood. Wriggling slightly nearer, and doing it so easily and gradually as not to attract the attention of the Mexican guard, Simms waited to see what would come of his officer's new move.

Slowly, diligently, Hal worked at the first knot. He felt a thrill of joy when his busy fingers untangled that knot. Then another one, and another one. Simms's wrists were free! The soldier, without attracting attention so far, moved himself slightly so as to bring his bound elbows within easy reach of Lieutenant Hal's fingers.

But there was no telling at what moment these fanatic Mexicans would discover what was going on, and balk it all.

Simms's wrists were free. Slowly, the soldier tried to repay his officer. Then Hal's wrists were free; then his elbows.

Two of the prisoners were now free, though they were careful not to move their arms in the least.

Yet how much had been gained? Two men there were who might leap up and fight for their lives. But they were unarmed, while the alert Mexicans had revolvers in their hands and dirks within instant reach.

Had either Hal or his man been able to roll over completely, one more comrade's knots would then be within reach. Yet, in rolling, either lieutenant or private would surely betray to the guards the fact that the cords were loosed from his arms. Nor could there be much doubt as to what the two desperate Mexicans would do in the face of any attempt at escape.

Hal lay there deliberating, trying to plan some move that would carry with it a reasonable prospect of victory. Simms, fearing to spoil any of his officer's plans, kept wholly silent, though alert for any signal.

"It's only the slimmest kind of a fighting chance yet!" muttered Hal. He would have been despondent, but his soldier's training had taught him that no situation is hopeless as long as life lasts.

Then craft, slowly, but insinuatingly, entered the young lieutenant's head.

"Confound you Mexicans," he growled aloud, "this is a bigger night for you than I had thought."

"What mean you?" demanded the guard who spoke English.

"I thought but one wagon train of your supplies would go to the water front this night."

"Eh?"

"And now, with my ear to the ground, I hear another lot of wagons in the distance, headed this way."

The guard looked non-plussed. He stood erect, listening. Then he spoke in Spanish to his fellow-Mexican, who, answering only with a nod, stepped further away to listen.

"I could tell you something, my friend, that it would be worth your while to know," continued Hal, craftily.

"What?"

"Only your ear shall hear it. Bend low, if you are curious."

The guard, without fear of the supposedly bound captive, stepped closer, bending over the young Army officer.

With a quick turn and a leap Hal Overton was up and at the throat of his captor. Taken so utterly by surprise the Mexican strove to leap back. But Hal had grappled with him and wrenched the revolver away. The Mexican reached for his handy knife. It was no time for niceties. Hal dealt the fellow a swift blow on top of his head with the butt of the revolver.

Mr. Mexican crumpled and lay where he had stood. But the other Mexican was closing in now.

"Get your hands up as high as you can, fellow!" ordered Hal. Just in the nick of time he remembered Captain Foster's instructions, and spoke in English instead of Spanish. But his gesture was eloquent enough for no words to be needed.

The second Mexican showed no cowardice, yet in this threatened battle at close quarters he dropped his revolver for the more trusted knife.

"Put your hands up and stop this nonsense!" commanded the young officer, stepping forward, holding the revolver at his belt, the muzzle covering the body of the swarthy foe.

The Mexican proved to possess no mean courage. With his knife-hand uplifted he sprang at Hal.

At that very instant a form hurled itself through the air. Private Simms fell at the feet of the Mexican. Without pause the soldier wrapped his arms about the Mexican's knees, throwing the fellow backward with jarring force. In another second Simms had possessed himself of the knife.

"Good!" came a devout chorus from the five bound but watching soldiers. "Great!"

"That was a fine specimen of soldierly wit and promptness, Simms," commended Lieutenant Hal heartily.

"Not half equal to what I've heard that you've done in the Philippines and elsewhere, sir," replied Simms modestly, as he seated himself on the fallen foe. "Will you take this knife, sir, and free the other men, or shall I leave this fellow in your care while I set the men free?"

"I'll free them," agreed Hal, taking the knife. Inside of a minute the young officer had five more serviceable soldiers at his orders.

"Now, lash these two rascals," commanded Lieutenant Overton. "This fellow, first, whom I was obliged to beat with his own revolver."

The tying was done by two of the soldiers. Then the wretch whom Simms bestrode was treated to some of the same sort of consideration. The pair of Mexicans were laid side by side, after which the soldiers sprang to get their cartridge belts and rifles.

"Check and Varnum, you two stay here with your prisoners, and give them no license to shout or pass signals. Check, fix your bayonet, and stand over these fellows. If either opens his mouth, shove your bayonet into it. Varnum, make it your business to watch over Check and see to it that he doesn't get the noose from behind, as all of us did once."

While speaking Lieutenant Overton was fastening on his own recovered revolver and cartridge box.

"Now, you other four men," he concluded, "come with me. Silence and soft steps must be our watchword. Unless we have the worst sort of evil luck we'll find out what's going on at the water front."

The distance was not great. Hal did not make the mistake of moving his abridged command of four men down the road. Instead they kept to the woods or behind bushes as much as they could.

As he came within sight of the water Lieutenant Hal held up his hand—a signal to halt. Then he peered through the darkness.

"Just about as I had supposed," he whispered. "Guarez has a tug in at the pier—a steam craft that will move out, as it came in, without lights."

"Queer, sir, that some of the other men haven't acted—they must have seen the tug come in."

"But I am supposed to be on duty in this neighborhood, and so are you men as sentries," whispered Lieutenant Overton. "Our other men, up the river and down, must imagine that we have taken care of the tug, if the craft needed such attention, and so the other men are holding their own posts according to their orders. Now, come on, men. Crouch low and make no noise. If you see me run for the pier follow without waiting for orders."

The military party succeeded in getting within a hundred and fifty yards of the land end of the pier. From here Hal could make out the figures of men lifting the last two cases to the deck of the tug.

At the same instant a man on the pier caught sight of the advancing soldiers. With a shrill whistle the fellow leaped to the deck of the tug, calling out to some one.

Without loss of a second Lieutenant Hal sprinted forward, dashing on to the pier.

In the engine room of the tug a single bell sounded—the moving signal. The last two cases had just been dumped on the deck, and two men leaped ashore, rushing for the shore-ends of the hawsers.

"Lift that hawser and I'll shoot you!" warned Lieutenant Hal.

"Who in blazes are *you*?" roared a deep, powerful voice from the deck of the tug.

"I'll ask the same question of you, sir," shot back Hal, running up.

"I'm the master of this tug, and *I* give the orders here!"

"I'm an officer of the United States Army, and your boat is undoubtedly to be seized by the government," Hal retorted.

The gang-plank had been drawn in, but Lieutenant Hal, measuring the distance with the eye of an athlete, leaped on to the deck.

Two of Hal's soldiers followed him aboard, the other two remaining on the pier.

"What's your name, sir?"

"Boggs," growled the master, a thick-set, powerful-looking, red-faced man of perhaps fifty. "What's yours?"

"I am Lieutenant Overton, of the United States Army," answered Hal.

Guarez and three other Mexicans ran out from the cabin and tried to leap ashore.

"Don't let these Mexicans get away if you have to shoot them down," Hal ordered quickly. "They're United States prisoners."

"This is a high-handed proceeding, Lieutenant," stormed Captain Boggs.

"Isn't it?" jeered Hal. Then, to the soldiers on the pier:

"Drive those two deckhands aboard, and stand ready to cast off, my men, when I give the order."

"What on earth are you up to here?" blustered Boggs.

"I'll tell you about that, sir, when I have time," Lieutenant Hal answered.

The two deckhands having come aboard sulkily, the soldiers stood by the hawsers.

"Cast off!" directed Hal. "Come on board, Captain Boggs. I'll trouble you to step into your own wheel-house."

Pedro Guarez stood by the low rail, in the way of the party's progress forward.

"Guarez, I'll trouble you to step aside."

The Mexican snarled, made a move as though to reach for his knife, then sullenly obeyed and stood aside.

At the door of his wheel-house Captain Boggs hesitated.

"I don't believe I'll go into the wheel-house," he growled.

"Guess again," rejoined Lieutenant Overton grimly. "Would you rather go in of your own accord, or be jabbed in there by a soldier's bayonet?"

"You've no right to take such high-handed action," snarled the master of the tug.

"You're in no position to decide that, Captain. You're a United States prisoner, at least until I have had opportunity to communicate with my superior officer. Go inside, sir."

Boggs obeyed, and Hal stationed a soldier at the wheel-house door.

"Now you Mexicans get back into the cabin," Hal continued, stepping back amidships.

"We're going ashore," snarled Pedro Guarez.

"You're going to *obey orders*," Lieutenant Hal retorted, "and I've ordered you into the cabin."

Instead Guarez turned as though he would leap ashore. The tug had now drifted some six feet from the string-piece of the pier.

"Squad, load!" ordered Hal sharply.

"Shoot if you dare!" challenged Guarez. "My friends and I are going ashore." Then he addressed a few words in Spanish to his friends. The words were so rapidly uttered that Overton could not understand them.

"Squad ready!" called Hal sternly. "Aim——"

To the ears of the Mexicans it sounded as though the word "fire" trembled on the young officer's lips. Guarez led the wild rush into the cabin.

Hal smiled. He had not had the least intention of firing upon the Mexicans. His seeming firmness had been enough.

"Close the cabin doors on both sides, and guard 'em," Lieutenant Overton directed. "Simms!"

"Yes, sir."

"Run back up the road and bring Check and Varnum, and their prisoners here without delay."

"Very good, sir."

Simms measured the distance to the string-piece with accuracy, then he made a leap and landed.

The engineer and fireman stood leaning out over the closed lower half of the engine-room door.

"What do you want us to do, General?" demanded the engineer, with a grin.

"Just stay where you are," Hal answered pleasantly. "Obey the bell-signals and keep steam up, and I don't believe you'll run into any hardship."

CHAPTER XV

TO OBEY ORDERS, OR NOT?

PRIVATE Simms soon returned, bringing with him Check and Varnum and the two Mexican prisoners. The Mexicans were forced to join their kind in the cabin, and Hal had two more soldiers to back his authority.

"Simms, hurry back to camp, looking out for the noose on the way. Report to Captain Foster what you've seen here, and inform him, with my compliments, that I await his further commands. This boat will wait at some distance out in the stream."

Just before Hal gave these instructions, Captain Boggs had been directed to run his boat back against the pier. Simms, saluting, stepped ashore and went off at brisk stride.

"One bell ahead, Captain," ordered Lieutenant Hal, showing his face at the wheel-house window.

"I don't know whether I'll do that or not," growled Boggs, filling a short, black pipe and lighting the tobacco.

"You'll either obey orders, sir, or you'll go back into the cabin with the Mexicans, and let your mate run the boat. If your mate refuses he'll join in the cabin and I'll do the best I can with the boat myself. Now, sir, are you going to obey orders?"

"Where do you want to go?" growled the riverman.

"One bell ahead."

"But where are you bound for?"

"That is none of your business, as you are no longer in command here. One bell ahead, sir."

Boggs looked as though he were going to balk flat, until he saw Hal turn as though to summon a soldier. Then the tug's master reached for the bell-pull. Clang! The tug's propeller began to churn slowly.

"Throw the wheel over two points to port," Hal continued. "Now, hold her steady ahead."

Still at half speed the craft moved out into the river some four hundred feet.

"Stop your speed, Captain."

Boggs obeyed, demanding next, "What now!"

"Nothing until I tell you," Lieutenant Hal responded.

"But the drift will carry us downstream."

"If we get too far down we'll steam back. Mate!"

"Aye, aye, sir," answered the man standing beside the tug's master.

"Get your masthead light out. Then display your starboard and port sidelights. Men," called Hal to his soldiers, "I call upon you to note and remember that this craft had no lights out until I ordered them out."

"We don't need lights out at the pier," growled Boggs, comprehending the meaning of Lieutenant Overton's remark.

"I believe you do," Hal rejoined, "when you are about to leave the pier for the stream. However, that's a point for higher authority than yours or mine to determine."

The mate soon had the running lights properly displayed and returned to the wheel-house.

Very slowly the boat drifted downstream. After fifteen minutes Hal directed that the skipper take his boat far enough upstream to make up for the drift.

From time to time the Army boy turned his gaze toward the pier. Hal had no need to bother himself with discipline aboard. All the crew and the Mexicans were confined where they could be watched, for the two deckhands were Mexicans, and had been driven in with the others. Five of Uncle Sam's soldiers were enough to keep the prize safe.

Lieutenant Overton was beginning to grow impatient when he saw a squad of troops, as he judged them to be in the darkness, march out on to the pier. Then the voice of Captain Foster hailed:

"Lieutenant Overton!"

"Here, sir."

"Bring that tug in."

"Very good, sir."

Hal gave the order to Captain Boggs, who sulkily obeyed. The mate was permitted to go aft and to bring two swarthy deckhands out where he could use them.

The boat was soon berthed, and hawsers made fast. Without waiting for the gang-plank to be placed Captain Foster sprang aboard, grasping his "youngster's" hand.

"Fine work, Mr. Overton!" commended the captain heartily.

"It came near being very bad work, sir."

"So I've gained from what Simms has told me on the way down here. But you showed the real commander, Mr. Overton, in your ability to extricate yourself from a bad mess and turn it into victory."

Captain Foster had brought with him a sergeant and ten men. There were now enough soldiers to post so that there need be no fear of any of the prisoners being able to escape.

"Sergeant, have two of the cases brought ashore," directed Captain Foster. "And open them."

Some of the cases were on the deck forward. Others had been dropped into a small hold forward.

The cases opened proved to contain rifles, ten to a case. Some smaller boxes from the hold were found to hold cartridges to fit the rifles.

"A very bad business for you, Boggs," remarked Captain Foster.

"Why is it?" demanded Boggs gruffly.

"You were going to smuggle these arms and supplies into Mexico, across the river."

"Where's your proof?" demanded the tug's master cunningly.

"Our Mexican prisoners are proof enough," replied the Army captain, with a shrug of his shoulders. "That and some of the other wild doings of to-night. Captain Boggs, you will prepare to accompany us back to camp."

"Why?"

"Because you're a prisoner, charged with conspiring to break the laws of the United States."

"But who'll look after my boat?" demanded Boggs.

"She'll be under guard of a squad of my men, and your mate, deckhands and engine-room force will be enough to give the boat any care she really needs. Mr. Overton, march the Mexicans out of the cabin under guard."

Hal promptly obeyed. Guarez and his companions appeared to be furious, and contended loudly that their rights were being infringed.

"That's all a matter for higher government authorities to settle," responded Captain Foster, with a shrug of his shoulders. "I cautioned you this morning, Guarez, against any enterprise of this sort, and you did not see fit to give my suggestion any consideration. You must now take the consequences. Sergeant Raney, take six men and escort the prisoners to camp. My compliments to Lieutenant Terry, and he is directed to take all precautions that the prisoners do not escape."

"Very good, sir."

After the escort had left with the prisoners Hal saluted his superior officer, asking:

"Sir, shall I re-post the sentries who were noosed and taken away from their posts?"

"It is hardly necessary, Mr. Overton. This boat is a government prize, and I propose to use her, for to-night at least, for the patroling of the river at this point. Mate, I see that you have a search-light."

"Yes, sir," the mate admitted.

"Is it ready for operation?"

"There is plenty of current, sir, and the lamp can be switched on from the wheel-house."

"Turn the light on once for a test, then."

The mate complied, sending a glare of light out over the dark waters.

"Switch the light off," called Captain Foster, next turning to remark to his young lieutenant:

"I don't want to let him manipulate that light enough to send any signals to possible Mexican watchers, Overton."

"I was just thinking of something of the sort, sir," Hal smiled. "And there's another puzzle in my mind. Have you any idea, sir, how these Mexicans got the cases out of Guarez's barn in spite of your guard at that point?"

"The cases didn't come from Guarez's barn," replied Captain Foster, with a laugh. "Do you begin to see light, Mr. Overton?"

"I believe I do, sir," muttered Lieutenant Hal. "The cases in Guarez's barn, it may be, are only dummies, put there with a good deal of display, so that if troops came their commander would be sure to hear about them. The Mexicans probably imagined that, after an American military commander came here, heard the gossip about boxes in Guarez's barn, and then guarded that barn, that the commander would then feel that all needed precautions had been taken. That was Mexican craft, but Guarez failed to understand that he was dealing with American thoroughness."

"That was about the size of the shallow trick the Mexicans tried on us," laughed Captain Foster.

"Are you going to send these cases ashore, sir?"

"Not until daylight. We must not forget that there may be another expedition attempted at some other point. Mr. Overton, I begin to think that this may be the point chosen for the shipment of arms enough for fitting out a whole rebel army

66

in Mexico. I think I will go back to camp, now, and question Guarez. I may find him in a mood to talk."

"And my orders, sir?"

"Make this boat your headquarters. Do not leave here until I return, Mr. Overton."

"Very good, sir."

"It was a pretty slick way that you caught us," began the mate, lounging near Hal as he stood on deck.

"Then you admit that this boat was engaged in an attempt at smuggling arms over the border?" demanded the young lieutenant, wheeling quickly.

"What's the use of denying it," questioned the mate, "with such cargo as we have?"

"Very little use indeed," Hal rejoined. "How much were you to get as your share of the night's work?"

"Oho! I didn't say that I had even a suspicion of what the game was," retorted the mate coolly. "I could only suspect, at best. You can't trap me into saying anything that would send me along to share Captain Boggs's fate."

"You're smooth enough," nodded Lieutenant Overton, "but don't try to play any further tricks."

"With United States troops aboard? What do you take me for?" grumbled the mate.

Hal didn't feel much inclined to talk with the fellow, so he stepped forward, leaving the mate by himself.

Half an hour passed. Truth to tell, the young Army officer felt the monotony of his present position, confined to the boat and the pier. Passing the sentry at the gang-plank, who stood at present arms in salute, Hal Overton walked forward to the outer end of the pier. He had stood there some ten minutes, when, two or three miles up the river, he thought he saw a brief flash.

"That might have come from a search-light, swiftly operated," thought Lieutenant Hal, with a start. After a moment's reflection, he hurried on board the boat.

"Mate," he directed, "shove off and steam out just past the end of the pier."

"Why——" began the mate wonderingly.

"Obey the order, sir!"

As the boat moved slowly into open water Hal, standing by the search-light, gave another order:

"Switch on this light, mate."

"But your captain said——"

"Switch on the light, man! Be quick about it!"

As the light gleamed out Lieutenant Hal turned its broad flare up the river. Just on the edge of the beam he picked up a motor boat of considerable size. The other craft was some three miles up the river, headed due south across to the Mexican border.

In the instant that the man in charge of the motor boat discovered the search-light, he crowded on more speed.

"My plain orders are to remain here," quivered Lieutenant Hal to himself. "If I obey, even during a five minutes' delay, that craft will outfoot us to Mexico, and a cargo of arms will be on the other shore. There's no time to communicate with Captain Foster. What on earth shall I do—disobey and face the chance of trial for disobedience of orders?"

CHAPTER XVI

AFTER SWIFT GAME

IT was a ticklish position, and one that called for quick decision.

If Lieutenant Overton ordered the tug back to the pier and remained where he was, he would be but obeying explicit orders. No blame could afterward attach to him, no matter how many boats got across.

At the same time the young Army officer knew that he was stationed here for the express purpose of preventing any arms being smuggled over to Mexico.

"Even though I capture a boat with ten thousand stands of arms aboard," flashed swiftly through the Army boy's mind, "Captain Foster can still say that I disobeyed orders. Yet if I obey orders there's no telling what mischief may be done."

"Yet it seems to me that, when I am set to watch a violation of the national law, my first duty is to try to catch any one who attempts to violate the law," quivered the lieutenant.

Suddenly Hal turned to the mate.

"Go ahead, man—full speed! Catch that boat yonder!"

No reply did the mate make, but he rang one bell for half-speed ahead. This he presently followed with the signal for full speed. The tug's propeller churned the water astern. For a craft of this kind the tug was now moving fast. Hal steadily held the ray of the search-light on the stranger.

"Can't you hump a little more speed out of this tub?" the young officer demanded.

"I can't signal for any more," replied the mate, his hands on the spokes of the wheel. "Why don't you ask the engineer?"

Young Overton quickly summoned a soldier and sent him to the engineer with a message calling for more speed. After another minute the increase in speed was easily discernible.

"But that boat's getting away from us," cried Lieutenant Overton, with irritation in his voice.

"Of course she is," spoke the mate gruffly. "I could have told you that she'd show us a clean pair of heels."

"What craft is she?"

"I don't know," the mate replied.

"Then how do you know she can beat us?"

"By her build. She's a costly gasoline boat, and such craft usually have high-power engines in 'em."

Hal sent another message to the engineer, who, however, sent back word that he was doing the best he could until draft made the fires under the boiler hotter.

"Is the engineer dealing frankly with me, mate?" Hal asked.

"I think he is. The engineer hasn't any object in seeing you lose this race."

"We're losing it all right, anyway," grunted the young officer, noting the rapidly increasing distance between pursuer and pursued.

"There ain't really any use in your trying to finish the race, sir?" hinted the mate.

"We'll keep it up to the end."

"Right to the Mexican shore?"

"If we have to," rejoined Hal. "We may at least overhaul that boat before it has all its cargo ashore."

"But you can't perform police duty on Mexican territory," urged the mate.

"True," replied Hal, biting his lip, for in his haste and eagerness he had overlooked that point of law.

"Besides," continued the mate, "you might butt right into a lot of assorted trouble. There may be a big force of Mexican rebels on hand to receive the arms. As they're already outlaws against their own government they would not hesitate about shooting into a small force of United States soldiers."

"My men are not cowards," uttered Hal. "They can shoot back, and straight enough, too."

"But you might be wiped out just the same, and, with you, the crew, who are not interested in such a fight."

"Nothing would stop me," retorted Hal, "if I had the legal right to pursue to the Mexican shore and make such a seizure there. But it's pretty clear to me that I have no such right, and that I'd only get into trouble with my own government, though really doing the government of Mexico a big favor."

"Then shall I put about, sir?" asked the mate.

"Not until you get the order plainly," Lieutenant Overton returned dryly. "I've heard of such things as gasoline boats breaking down. The boat we're after may have that kind of luck before she gets out of United States jurisdiction."

No such fortune for the young soldier happened, however. The gasoline boat, still followed by the rays of light from the tug, entered a cove on the Mexican side. Hal turned the light full on some moving objects on the bank of the cove. A score of figures were dancing there, and shouting derisively at the out-distanced American tug. From where he stood forward Hal could make out other men hurriedly lifting cases to the shore.

"You got the best of us, for once, you brown-faced men," Hal laughed. "Head about, mate. We can do no good here. Do you recognize that motor boat yet?"

"I do not, of course, and I note that her name has been removed from under the stern."

Having turned about the mate headed back for the village of Agua Dulce.

Just as the tug was making in at the village pier, Hal descried the figure of Captain Foster just stepping on to the pier.

"My captain won't keep me guessing long, if he's really displeased," reflected Hal, with an inward quiver.

"Tug ahoy, there!" hailed Captain Foster in a displeased voice.

"Ahoy, sir!" Hal shouted back.

"Haven't you been away out in the stream, sir?"

"Yes, sir."

Captain Foster asked no more for the moment, so Hal offered no further information.

On the instant, however, when the deckhands leaped ashore with the hawse-lines Captain Foster called quietly, even if coldly:

"Come ashore, Mr. Overton, as soon as you can."

"Now I rather reckon I'm in for it," thought the young lieutenant, ruefully, though he was really torn with the fear that he had exceeded his own authority to a dangerous point.

CHAPTER XVII

THE THIRTY-FOURTH JOINS HANDS

CAPTAIN FOSTER, too just a man to condemn without a hearing, let his young officer explain at length. All through this the older man preserved an unchanged countenance.

"Mr. Overton," spoke the captain, at last, "had I thought it likely that you would have such an experience, I would have given you leave to pursue in such a case. As I did not give such permission your conduct amounted to a breach of orders. At the same time, it was a breach very likely to be committed by a younger officer, and the intentions back of your conduct were unquestionably good and for the best interests of our mission here. I shall, therefore, neither approve nor disapprove of your conduct. I will add only the hint that, at another time, you will do well to stick literally to the orders you receive. To that advice there is only one exception. In spite of the orders you would have been fully at liberty to have moved your position had the lives of your men been needlessly and senselessly exposed by remaining. Such, however, was not the case."

"May I speak, sir?" inquired Hal.

"Certainly, Mr. Overton."

"If my conduct amounted to a fault, sir, it was not a deliberate one. I debated with myself as fully as I could in the few moments that were left to me in which to come to any decision. It seemed to me, sir, that my duty lay in chasing that motor boat. I feel, Captain, that my greatest fault was in judgment, and I had no experience to guide me in the matter."

"Your defense is a very manly one, Mr. Overton. I like you better for the way you have stated it."

"I trust, sir, that the mistake I have made to-night will not lessen your confidence in me, hereafter."

"It will not," replied Captain Foster heartily, holding out his hand. "And now, let us say no more about it. You were not able to make out the name of the boat, but you must have had a good look at her for descriptive purposes."

"Not very, sir; the boat had canvas over its woodwork. I am afraid, sir, that, if I saw the same boat in daylight, I couldn't positively identify her."

"We have duties to perform, now, Mr. Overton. Instruct your sergeant that he is, under no circumstances, to allow the tug to leave the pier, except under orders. Then come with me."

A minute later Hal and his superior officer were walking briskly up the street.

"There's a telephone cable under the river to Tres Palmas," explained Captain Foster. "You will therefore call up the operator there, and you will explain to-night's incident of the motor boat, and ask him to notify the Mexican federal authorities. That's all that's left to us now. While you are doing that I will telephone both up and down the river, calling on the state authorities to seize that fast motor boat, if they can catch it on the American side."

The telephone messages were sent, and the two officers retraced their way to the tug. The message that went under the river to Mexico, as Captain Foster learned long afterward, did not reach the federal government of that sister republic, for the telephone office, for three hours that night, was held by a roving band of Mexican rebels who succeeded in intercepting many government messages and in learning the plans of the Mexican government for crushing these same rebels.

"Mr. Overton," said Hal's superior officer, when they reached the boat, "you will find berths in the cabin of the boat. Get into one of them and sleep until breakfast-time unless you are called earlier. I will now make myself responsible for the watch along the river."

It was full breakfast-time, at eight in the morning, therefore, when one of the soldiers touched Hal on the shoulder.

"Captain Foster's compliments to Lieutenant Overton, who is directed to report on deck to the captain."

"Mr. Overton," announced the superior officer, as soon as his "youngster" appeared on deck, "I am going up to the camp for the day, unless you send me word that I am needed. I have just breakfasted, and the cook of this craft will take your orders as to your own breakfast."

"Have the men breakfasted, sir?" was Hal's first thought and question. A really good officer always thinks first of his men.

"They have all breakfasted, Mr. Overton. I do not imagine you will have much to do in the day-time. You have only your boat guard of six men under Sergeant Raney. The water-front patrol I have called in and sent to camp."

Hal ate his breakfast in leisurely fashion. He had slept well and was refreshed, but he believed that he had a long and dull day before him. And so it proved. The day passed on with absolutely nothing to do but eat and lounge, save for the one sentry who watched both boat and shore end.

It was almost dark, and Hal had just seated himself in the cabin to eat his supper when the sentry hailed:

"Lieutenant Overton!"

Hal showed his head at the cabin door.

"A detachment of troops approaching, sir."

"Well, they're our own men, aren't they, sentry?" Hal inquired.

"I think not, sir."

Hal stepped back into the cabin, picked up and donned his cap, then stepped out on deck. The approaching troops were on the dock by the time that the young lieutenant had returned to the open.

"Two officers and ten men!" flashed through Hal's mind.

Then, of a sudden, he felt like giving a whoop of joy. Instead, however, he darted down the gang-plank, then caught himself and walked forward with dignity just as one of the approaching officers called out with military crispness:

"Squad halt! Break ranks!"

"Mr. Prescott! Mr. Holmes!" cried Hal, going up to the two lieutenants who had just arrived.

"Hullo, Overton," responded both newly-arrived officers, extending their hands, while Prescott added:

"By Jove, I didn't count on finding you here, though I heard that you had won your commission. Where's Terry?"

"Up at our camp, Mr. Prescott."

"Drop the formal 'Mr.,' Overton, do," urged Lieutenant Prescott. "We have known each other long enough not to stand on ceremony."

"We've known each other in other times," laughed Holmes, "and in much more stirring times, I take it, than these are likely to be."

"Don't be too sure about the present being tame times," urged Hal. "From what we have seen here so far I believe that we are right in the middle of a district that is heavily engaged in sending arms over into Mexico. We may have a fight with a lot of these desperate, fanatic Mexican rebels at any moment."

"Let it come, then," laughed Holmes indifferently. "We need a bit of practice, now and then, to keep us in handy touch with our work."

"But how does the Thirty-fourth happen to be down here?" Hal asked curiously.

"Ordered away from Fort Clowdry. That's all I know," Prescott answered. "At least B and C companies were sent. We detrained at Spartansburg, eighteen miles from here. The two companies are now about six miles above, save for this little detachment, which was sent down to report to Captain Foster for some co-operation with you on the water."

"Lieutenant," spoke a sergeant of B company, approaching and saluting, "may I ask, sir, whether the men are to eat field rations or whether they're to be fed on the boat?"

"What do you say, Overton? How much food is there on the boat?"

"I'll find out from the cook," Hal answered. "Sergeant Kelly, are you going to forget me in that fashion?"

"You're an officer now, sir," replied Sergeant Kelly, saluting. "I awaited your pleasure, sir, about speaking."

"I can't see that you've changed any, Sergeant," smiled Hal, extending his hand. "But for the difference in some of the stage-settings we might seem to be in the Philippines instead of in Texas."

"This is 'God's country,' sir," replied Kelly, with an air almost of reverence. "There's nothing in the Philippines as restful to the eye as the meanest stretch in the United States."

Only a few months before while Hal and Noll were still in the Philippines Kelly had been made a corporal. Kelly was one of the staunchest souls in the Army. Many a time had he, with Noll and Hal, braved death side by side when facing the treacherous Moros. Since that time he had won the higher grade of sergeant.

"I'm heartily glad to see you again, Sergeant Kelly," Hal went on.

"Not more, sir, I'll be bound, than I am to see yourself," rejoined the sergeant.

Then, with a final salute, Kelly fell back, muttering to himself:

"'Tis come, the time when I must be saying 'sir' to two broths of boys that I've cooked bacon and coffee with over the same fire. But I don't begrudge either boy his honors. The two of them, they're the best of fine soldiers and true."

Hal hurriedly learned from the tug's cook that the provisions on board were equal to furnishing all the newly arrived soldiers with breakfast within an hour.

"And can I serve the two officers now with you, if you want, Lieutenant," said the cook.

"Then please do so."

Hal led his two brother-officers to the cabin, where Prescott and Holmes, after having removed their swords and belts, made hasty toilets and seated themselves.

"I imagine a good many more commands will be ordered into the field," Prescott continued. "Every few years a lot of discontented fellows over in Mexico start some kind of a revolution, but this present one appears to be the strongest one yet. Colonel North, I know, had a report to the effect that Mexicans enough were waiting on the other side of the river to organize a large army corps as soon as they can get guns enough from this side."

"Any arms captured on this side, yet, that you know of, Overton?"

"No," Hal answered. "But I guess a cargo got across all right. We got this boat, and a lot of cases on board, but the cases have been carted up to camp. If the cases have been opened yet I haven't heard what they contained."

"Arms or ammunition, or both, undoubtedly," nodded Lieutenant Holmes. "The Mexicans would hardly go to the trouble of sending a cargo of anything else out in the dead of night."

"Yes; I imagine they were arms, but I don't want to say so. Captain Foster did find war supplies in two of the cases that he opened, I ought to add. But I guess I've been rattled by meeting you two so unexpectedly."

"Getting rattled is a highly unmilitary form of conduct," retorted Prescott, with a look of mock sternness.

While the young officers were still at the table Captain Foster boarded and entered the cabin.

"Keep your seats, gentlemen," directed Captain Foster, throwing himself into a corner seat. "I've just eaten. Mr. Overton, your present detachment will march ashore presently, when a sergeant and nine men relieve them here. The two companies of the Thirty-fourth are to watch the water front to the west of us. When you go on the water to-night you'll carry officers and men from both regiments. If you have to land anywhere within the territory guarded by the Thirty-seventh, Mr. Overton, you'll be in command. If within the territory of the

73

Thirty-fourth Mr. Prescott is detailed by Captain Cortland to command on landing. While pursuing on the water, Mr. Overton, you will be in command at all times, as our regiment is furnishing the boat. Mr. Terry will accompany you also."

"There's a Navy officer, Ensign Darrin, who was visiting at Fort Clowdry, and who accompanied us, sir," announced Lieutenant Prescott. "Mr. Darrin stopped up in the village for supper and to send a telegram or two. If Mr. Darrin reaches us here in time, sir, I request permission to take him on board as a passenger."

"Who's taking my name in vain?" demanded a hearty voice from the cabin doorway.

Ensign Dave Darrin, U. S. N., as fine a looking young naval officer as ever trod bridge or quarter-dock, stood looking in.

"Come in, Darrin," cried Prescott, leaping up and moving forward. "Captain Foster, permit me to present Mr. Darrin, of the Navy."

Captain Foster made Darrin wholly welcome in a few words.

"Hullo, Overton. Where's Terry?" cried Ensign Dave.

More greetings were in order.

"Just as you announced yourself, Mr. Darrin," said Captain Foster, "Mr. Prescott was asking permission to take you on the water as a passenger to-night. I beg to assure you that you will be most heartily welcome to go anywhere with this very small slice of the Army."

Darrin expressed his thanks.

Readers of the third volume of this series are sure to remember Ensigns Darrin and Dalzell, then midshipmen, who visited Prescott and Holmes in the Rocky Mountains and took part in a famous hunting trip. Hal and Noll, then sergeants, then made their first acquaintance with Darrin and Dalzell.

All readers of the "High School Boys' Series" know full well that Darrin and Dalzell were famous members of the Dick & Co. of bygone school days, while readers of the "Annapolis Series" have followed Dave and Dan all through their days at the United States Naval Academy.

"As all you youngsters know each other from old times I fancy you'll have a most agreeable time on the water to-night, if there proves to be nothing to do but swap yarns of former days," smiled Captain Foster.

"Don't you go with us on the water, sir!" inquired Ensign Darrin.

"No; I am on shore. Mr. Overton, however, will give the best account of my hospitality that the limited resources of this boat permit."

"Where's Mr. Dalzell?" asked Lieutenant Hal, as he finished his coffee.

"Why, he's up at Fort Clowdry—waiting—to—well, I guess I'll let Prescott tell it," finished Ensign Dave.

For some reason Prescott blushed slightly, opened his mouth as though to speak, and then failed to do so. The reason for his confusion will appear later.

By this time darkness had come on, and the cook, who was also the only cabin attendant, had switched on the electric lights in the snug cabin. The young officers, however, felt that they had so many matters to discuss that the deck would give them more room, so they adjourned.

Some of the officers noted that Captain Foster frequently glanced down the river through the darkness, but none asked him his reasons.

Finally, however, Sergeant Havens and ten men from F company marched on to the pier, followed by Corporal Shimple of H company and four men. In the wake of the two detachments walked Lieutenant Noll, who was soon shaking hands heartily with three of his brother officers of the United Services.

"May I ask what you see coming, gentlemen?" inquired Captain Foster, suddenly, pointing down the river.

"It looks like some pirate craft, sir," replied Hal, after peering hard through the darkness. "At least, that seems like a fair guess, for she's moving along without lights."

"She's engaged in United States service of a somewhat stealthy nature," replied Captain Foster. "That's why the craft shows no lights. Mr. Overton, how do you like the idea that you're to command a gasoline boat yourself to-night, and one that is reputed to be exceedingly fast?"

Hal Overton felt a sudden glow of exultation as the situation dawned on his mind.

"I wired, last night, for a fast gasoline boat to be sent here to aid us," continued Captain Foster. "This coming craft is the answer to my prayer, and the nearest collector of customs informs me that she's the swiftest thing he could charter for the government in these waters."

"Then, sir, if the Mexicans try to put their motor boat across the river to-night there'll be some real doings!" promised Lieutenant Overton.

"Real doings," indeed! The border excitement was about to break loose in deadly earnest, but that was more than any of them knew at that time.

CHAPTER XVIII

AN ACT OF PIRACY

MOVING slowly, with the graceful ease of a monster swan, the motor boat, a craft under sixty feet in length, moved into the pier to shoreward of the tug.

"Motor boat 'Restless'?" hailed Captain Foster.

"Yes, sir," came quietly from the youthful-looking sailor at the wheel. Just then he quitted his post.

"Captain Halstead?"

"Yes, sir; here, at your orders."

Skipper Tom Halstead made the best military salute that he knew how, while the handy boy of all things aboard the boat, Hank Butts, made the bow-hawser fast and hurried along the pier to secure the stern hawser.

"A party of five United States officers coming aboard, Captain Halstead," continued Captain Foster.

"All right, sir; we'll be mighty glad to have you aboard," Skipper Tom answered quietly, but with a manliness and heartiness that made all of the officers instantly take a liking to him.

75

Captain Foster introduced himself, and then his brother officers. Many of our readers will require no new introduction to Captain Tom Halstead, Engineer Joe Dawson and the irrepressible trouble-seeker, Hank Butts. These fortunate readers have already met the young men in the volumes of the "Motor Boat Club Series," and know all about them and how Tom and Joe had secured their joint ownership in that splendid sea-going craft, the "Restless."

"Halstead, can you take five officers and twenty enlisted men aboard for the night?"

"Yes, sir," smiled the young skipper, revealing his white, even teeth. "They won't weigh over two tons and a half, altogether, sir."

"Can you take that many with comfort?" laughed Captain Foster.

"Now, I won't guarantee the comfort, sir, but there'll be room enough aboard so that no one needs to be jostled over the rail. Eighteen men can sit in the cabin at the same time. That leaves only seven, besides our own crew who will need to be on deck."

"Oh, you're going to have plenty of room here," decided Captain Foster, after a brief look over the trim little motor craft.

"I'm glad of that," sighed Dave Darrin, "for, as an interloper, I'd have to go ashore the first one if the quarters were crowded."

"Mr. Overton, direct Sergeant Havens and his men to come aboard. Mr. Prescott, you'll look out for your squad, of course."

"Certainly, sir."

"Mr. Overton, as soon as you have your men aboard, give the skipper his word to start. You will cruise without lights, unless need for them arises. While cruising, do not go above nine miles an hour. Reserve greater speed for pursuit. First, you will cruise eight miles up the river, then eight miles below this point, and so on through the night until a half-hour before daylight. As much as you can, avoid showing your craft to any prowlers by the shores. Keep things dark aboard the boat, and voices low."

By this time the enlisted men had come aboard, many of them going below to the cabin.

"You may start, now," continued Captain Poster, jumping to the pier. "Catch anything you can that has arms aboard for the other frontier. Good-bye and good luck!"

Hardly had the motor boat gotten under way when the tug, with Corporal Shimple and four men aboard, also left her berth. The tug went only a short distance out into the stream, then cast anchor for the night. The tug was to be held in reserve, and at the same time her mate and crew were thus prevented from communicating any news about the motor boat to possible Mexican lurkers on shore.

The five young officers of the two services had seated themselves on top of the deck-house at the rear of the bridge-deck. Hank Butts sat midway down on the deck-house, yawning as though he would like to turn in. After he had got his engine working smoothly Engineer Joe Dawson came up from the engine room forward, taking his stand beside Skipper Tom Halstead.

For five minutes Joe was silent, as the boat kept on up the Rio Grande. He half-turned, once in a while, to cast a covertly-admiring glance at the young officers seated at their rear. At last Joe whispered exultantly in his chum's ear:

"Tom, that's a real fighting bunch."

"You've hit the truth at first trial," returned Skipper Tom, in an undertone, as he kept his glance ahead over the river.

"I'm not much given to exaggeration, am I, Tom?"

"I never knew that you had an acquaintance with exaggeration," Halstead answered.

"Then perhaps you'll believe me, Tom, when I tell you that I'd follow those officers over Niagara or into Vesuvius, if they happened to be bound either way."

"I know you would, Joe," Tom answered, without smiling, for he knew his chum through and through.

"Tom, those young officers would *assay up a big lot of fight to the ton*!"

Having thus relieved himself of that strong conviction Joe Dawson seated himself on the roof of the forward house and did not speak again for twenty minutes.

By the time that the eight miles upstream had been covered, and Skipper Tom Halstead had headed the boat down again for its straight sixteen-mile run, he called down to his chum:

"Joe, will you come up and hold the wheel for me for two or three minutes?"

"Coming," Dawson sang cheerily.

But Dave Darrin stepped forward with:

"Skipper, can't *I* hold the wheel for you?"

"Have you ever handled a boat before, sir?" Tom queried, giving this young man, who was in civilian dress, a keen though good-humored look.

"At least twice," Darrin modestly assured him.

"How big a boat?"

"Up to sixteen thousand tons," Darrin replied, without cracking a smile.

"A wise man is always cautious, Halstead," sang out Lieutenant Prescott gleefully, "but the man you're talking to is Ensign Darrin of the United States Navy."

"Take the wheel, Mr. Darrin," replied the youthful skipper, with a grin, while Joe, halfway up the engine-room steps, took in the scene. "I heard Mr. Darrin introduced merely as 'mister,'" Halstead explained to the other officers. "I thought he was either an Army man, or some civilian friend who had come along."

Skipper Tom Halstead then went below to his stateroom, while observant Joe Dawson noted that Darrin handled the wheel with skill.

"Shall I give you a little more speed, Mr. Darrin?" called Joe softly.

"I'm only a guest," Dave replied. "Mr. Overton is in command here."

"Thank you, Engineer, but, as we're only cruising I believe our best move will be to stick to Captain Foster's nine-mile order," Hal replied, nodding to Joe.

So the cruise continued. Halstead was soon on deck again, but the young skipper found Darrin so enjoying his trick at the wheel that Skipper Tom merely

77

stood near to take the trick again whenever the young ensign showed signs of being tired of his job.

It was late in the night, and the "Restless" was making her third trip up the river before anything happened. For some time the young Army and Navy officers had felt more or less bored with the monotony of these hours of tiresome waiting. Tom Halstead had stretched himself out on the deck-house for rest, though not to nap, and Hank Butts was at the wheel, while Joe dozed lightly on a seat in the engine-room. All of the enlisted men had crowded below, and were dozing.

"Look sharp, there!" cried Lieutenant Hal, suddenly, as he sprang to Hank's side. "There's a craft moving out from the American shore, about a mile upstream, isn't there!"

"Something moving, for sure," replied Hank, peering through the darkness.

"A motor boat?"

"It must be."

"Trail her. Get in closer."

Skipper Tom Halstead now came forward, though he did not take the wheel from Hank.

"The search-light is ready, whenever you want it, Lieutenant," remarked the youthful motor boat skipper.

"The use of the light might save the fellows on the other craft some guessing," smiled Lieutenant Hal. "I want to keep 'em guessing as long as possible."

"I'll kick on more speed," proposed Hank, reaching for the deck controls.

"Wait until you get orders," interposed Skipper Tom Halstead. "This is government business, Hank, and we're not government officers, so we'll act only under orders."

It was evident that those aboard the craft upstream had made out the pursuing motor boat. The unknown craft was now heading straight across the stream, and kicking on some speed.

"How fast is the stranger going?" asked Lieutenant Overton.

"Twenty miles an hour, as nearly as I can guess," replied Skipper Tom.

"How fast can you go?"

"Twenty-six to twenty-eight miles."

"Crowd it about all on, then. I don't want to have that other craft get too close to Mexico before we push up alongside."

"All speed, Joe, and do it quick!" Skipper Tom called down into the engine-room. Almost at once the "Restless" earned her name by fairly leaping forward through the water.

Then the chase began in earnest.

"Noll, pass the word below for a sergeant and six privates," directed Lieutenant Hal, in a low tone.

The enlisted men came up, taking their places on deck.

"Does the lieutenant want us to load our pieces?" called the sergeant quietly.

"Not yet," was Hal's reply, passed back by Noll.

Then, on board the pursuing craft, all settled down to absolute quietness, save for the running of the machinery. The distance between the two boats was rapidly closing up, for it was plain that the other boat had started at full speed as soon as she sighted the pursuer.

Glare! A strong, broad beam of light, from the stranger's search-lamp, shone across the water, then picked up the "Restless" when the two boats were less than a quarter of a mile apart. The uniforms of Uncle Sam's blinking men must have stood out strongly before the vision of those on the stranger.

"You have a megaphone?" asked Lieutenant Hal.

"Yes," replied Skipper Tom, passing the implement.

"Run up just as close as you can safely for a hail."

Lieutenant Hal waited until much more of the distance had been covered. Then he raised the megaphone to his lips, shouting:

"Lay to, stranger! We are United States officers and must come aboard!"

"You can't!" bellowed a hoarse, defiant voice.

"We *must* and will! Lay to!"

"Take the consequences, then!" came the same hoarse bellow.

Bang! It came altogether, in one sharp, crashing volley, from the stranger's decks, and a tempest of bullets hit the "Restless."

"The pirates!" uttered Lieutenant Hal, at a white heat of indignation.

CHAPTER XIX

RASCALS AND MONEY TALK

HAL turned quickly, to see if any of his men had been hit.

"Not one hit, but it's a wonder," Noll informed his brother officer. "The bullets of those fellows made a pin-cushion of the air all about us."

"Ready, men! Load, aim!" ordered Lieutenant Overton. Then he added, in a lower voice:

"If I give the word 'fire,' be sure you sweep that stranger's deck clean."

"Don't you dare fire on us," yelled the same hoarse voice. "There are ladies aboard!"

"A likely yarn!" Hal jeered hotly.

"If you fire you'll find that there are. Now, sheer off!"

"You lay to," insisted Lieutenant Hal. "We're coming aboard."

"You only think you are!"

"Will you lay to?"

"No!"

"Run up alongside. We'll have to board 'em under way," Hal said, in a low voice. "Noll, head the men in the cabin. Order 'em to fix their bayonets. Don't bring them on deck until you find that we're boarding. Then be brisk about it!"

As the "Restless" leaped in to lay alongside the stranger there could no longer be any doubt as to the grim intentions of the United States forces.

From the deck of the stranger came another sheet of flame. Hal felt one of the bullets tear through his left sleeve, though without cutting the flesh of his arm.

"Fire!" he gave the order.

When they shoot, regulars are taught to do it coolly and with effect. Two or three yells from the stranger's deck greeted the volley, indicating that some had been hit.

But above all there rose a woman's piercing shriek.

"They really have a woman on board!"

gasped Hal, feeling chill and sick for an instant.

"Yes, you infernal scoundrels!" came in the same hoarse voice. "Oh, you'll pay for this outrage!"

"Fix bayonets!" Hal ordered, quietly, for now the two boats were close together, and Helmsman Hank was running the "Restless" right in for a boarding.

Bump! The two boats came together.

"Prepare to board! Board!" shouted Hal, and was first to leap to the deck of the stranger, a craft some seventy feet in length and rather broad of beam.

His soldiers followed him. All the young officers went over the side, and Lieutenant Noll led the reserves from the cabin of the "Restless."

Right on the heels of the soldiers followed Skipper Tom and Engineer Joe, to lash the two craft fast.

"Who commands here?" demanded Lieutenant Overton.

There was no answer.

"Where's the gentleman with the fog-horn voice who appeared to have so much to say?" Hal questioned sharply.

None of the crew of the boarded vessel spoke. Nor was any further effort at resistance made.

On the deck Lieutenant Overton found one Mexican dead, and another badly wounded. Near each lay a rifle. Another Mexican seemingly unarmed, stood by the wheel, looking on with a sickly grin, but saying nothing. Down in the engine-room huddled two other Mexicans.

"Sergeant, search the man at the wheel, and then the pair down in the engine-room," Hal ordered. "If you find weapons on them, make the men your prisoners."

Followed by Noll and a few enlisted men, the Army boy made his way aft to the entrance to the main cabin. Hal tried the door, but it resisted his efforts.

"Open this door," he called, "and save us the trouble of breaking it in."

"Don't dare break it in," remonstrated the hoarse voice. "If you do it will fall across the body of the woman you've probably already killed by your bullets."

Hal felt another chill run down his spine, but he answered firmly:

"If there's a wounded woman in there we'll do our best to rush her toward surgical help. But you'll have to open that door, or we'll do it for you!"

"Then you'd better stand away, boy!" warned the hoarse voice grimly. "If you try to force your way in here you'll eat more bullets than you'll like."

"Just what we're after," retorted Lieutenant Overton grimly. "We want to lay our hands on the men who fired on United States troops, and I know they must be in there, for they're nowhere else on the boat. Your deck holds only two out of all who fired. Going to open?"

"*No*, you young hound!"

"Put your shoulders to the door, men!" continued Hal, turning to the nearest soldiers.

"I'll shoot the first man who comes through!" defied the voice behind the door, hoarser than ever. "And I'll shoot as many more as I can!"

"Some of you men on the sides of the deck-house push your rifles through the cabin windows and be prepared to shoot if you have to," ordered Hal coolly.

There was a crashing of glass as the rifle muzzles were thrust in through the cabin windows.

Again the woman's shriek rang out.

"If you have to fire," continued Lieutenant Overton, "take all possible care not to hit the woman."

Bump! Bump! Even the sturdy cabin door was beginning to yield under the repeated impacts of so many pairs of shoulders. At last the door swung back on its hinges.

"Back, men, but stand ready!" commanded the Army boy, pressing forward through the opened doorway.

The handsome young lieutenant looked cool and undaunted as he stepped into the cabin, without a weapon in either hand.

Hal found himself confronted by a big, purple-faced individual of perhaps middle age, who stood glaring at the intruder, a revolver clutched in his right hand.

Back of him stood five Mexicans, each with a rifle, though the man at the moment was making no visible attempt to use his weapon. Behind the group a white-faced young woman, of perhaps twenty, stood clutching at a buffet for support.

"I think you had a wager on that you'd shoot me," smiled Lieutenant Hal. "Instead, be good enough to hand your pistol to the sergeant."

"I'll——"

"You'll give your weapon up," Hal continued smilingly. "Sergeant, relieve the gentleman of his pistol. He's too nervous to have one; he might discharge it accidentally."

The purple-faced fellow, who was evidently an American, opened his mouth as if to pour out a torrent of abuse. But the sergeant quietly wrenched the weapon from his hand.

"Now, you Mexicans lay your rifles down on the floor," Hal continued, turning to the swarthier men.

Hesitatingly they obeyed, for they realized that all hope of successful resistance was now gone.

"What relation is this young lady to you, if any?" Hal asked, turning to the man.

"He's my father," spoke the girl, instead.

"Then, madam, he may remain in the cabin with you, if he chooses. Sergeant, clear all others out of the cabin."

"What do you think you are going to do here, you young counter-jumper?" snarled the girl's father.

"We are going to take this craft and all it holds back to Agua Dulce as a prize," Hal replied quietly. "Madam, you were not wounded in the least, were you?"

"No," she answered, looking rather sheepish.

"Then we shall not need to make so much haste on your account. But we have a Mexican up on the deck who may need attention in a hurry."

"The fellow on the deck is only a Mexican," sneered the purple-faced one, all of his recent Mexican companions having been removed from the cabin by the soldiers.

"He's a badly wounded man, whether he's an American, Mexican, Chinaman or Hindu," Hal retorted. "All men are entitled to humane treatment by soldiers. And I think I hardly need to remind you, sir, that you yourself have deemed it worth while to be associated with Mexicans."

"Because business made it necessary," replied the American huskily, yet in a lower voice. "Almost every dollar I have in the world is invested in a part of Mexico that the *insurrectos* hold and seem likely to go on holding."

"The same old dollar excuse?" demanded Lieutenant Overton. "Are you another of the men who have grown to think that the straight and narrow path is found only in the space between the two parallel lines of the dollar-sign?"

Then, turning, Hal went to the door of the cabin to call:

"Lieutenant Terry!"

"Here, sir."

"Be good enough to inspect the cargo that this craft may carry, as speedily as you can. But we will begin here, and see what these piles are that have been covered with canvas at the forward end of the cabin."

"Rifle cases, beyond any doubt," nodded Noll, as he and Hal switched away the canvas covers.

"Cases that appear built to hold rifles and ammunition, up forward, Overton," called Prescott, coming to the cabin door.

"Yes; this boat is a gun-smuggler beyond a doubt," nodded Lieutenant Hal. "Even if we found no guns aboard we could hold the craft for a pirate, for the conduct of her commander in having his fellows fire on us."

"A pirate? Father, is that true?" called the young woman, in a startling voice.

"Hush, child. You don't understand such things," replied the man.

"But, if this be true? Oh, I must get out of here and get air. I am stifling."

"I shall be glad to assist you to the deck, madam, if you will permit me," offered Prescott, gravely, removing his cap.

At an almost imperceptible sign from her father the girl quickly moved forward and vanished with Lieutenant Prescott.

"I take it you're in command here," muttered the father.

"I am," Hal nodded.

"Then I want to talk with you," continued the stranger. "Lieutenant, of course I know that you've got me in a nasty position. I want to see how you can help me to get out of it."

"If you really are in a bad position," Hal responded, gazing into the other's eyes, "I do not see how I can help you, for I am only the officer concerned with seizing this craft. I am not going to be your judge."

"Oh, yes, you can," continued the other, sinking his voice still lower. "We can fix it all, I know, with money!"

CHAPTER XX

AN OFFICER AND HIS HONOR

"I'M afraid you're as badly off as the hunter's dog," observed Lieutenant Hal coldly.

"How is that?"

"You're barking up the wrong tree."

The purple-faced man looked searchingly into the clear, steady eyes of the young Army officer. Then he answered laughingly:

"Oh, come, now. Don't try to keep me guessing too long, or I may lose my patience, and you may lose some money that you'd rather have. Up forward there's a stateroom, and the light is turned on in there. Just step into the stateroom, by yourself, and count—this."

From a trousers pocket the purple-faced one had drawn a huge roll of bank-notes. Before Hal Overton could understand what was happening the stranger had pushed this roll of money into the young officer's hand.

"That's only a starter—something down to prove good faith, you understand," whispered the stranger.

"You—you *dog*!" cried Lieutenant Hal angrily.

Swat! The compact roll of bank-notes struck the stranger in the face, then bounded to the floor at Hal's feet. The latter kicked the money away from him.

"You needn't be so huffy about it," grumbled the other. "As I told you, that money is only a deposit paid down."

"You'll go down, if you try anything more like that," uttered Lieutenant Hal wrathfully.

"Ah, now, see here, don't be a fool," urged the stranger huskily. "I don't want to spend a lot of time behind bars or too much in the courts either. Now, all you'll have to do will be to help me frame a yarn that we can both——"

"Stop! I think I've heard about enough from you," warned Lieutenant Overton angrily.

"But, you idiot, I can offer you more money than you'll make in twenty years of soldiering!"

"Perhaps you can, but you needn't bother. Do you imagine, fellow, that an Army officer's honor is of so little importance to him that he'll sell it to a higher bidder. Now, I've had enough of you. Get out of here."

As Hal spoke he unfastened his belt and tossed it on to a seat at the side. It was his intention to call his brother officers into the cabin during the trip back. But at that moment Noll showed in the doorway.

"Lieutenant Overton, Mr. Halstead is inquiring whether you are ready with further orders."

That brought Hal to his feet, and also to the realization that both motor boats would have to be manned. Indeed, he would have to give a few moments of thought about the return to the American shore.

Hastily joining his brother officers on deck, Hal also called to Prescott, who placed a chair for the young woman and then joined the group.

"Prescott," Hal began, "I don't imagine that the capture of this craft is warrant for our abandoning river guard for the rest of the night. The 'Restless,' I take it, must continue the patrol until other orders are received."

"Undoubtedly," nodded Prescott.

"Therefore, it's my intention, with a few of our men, to take this prize into Agua Dulce. The remainder of the officers and men ought to remain aboard the 'Restless.' Now, as that boat belongs to the Thirty-seventh for the present I shall have to leave Terry in command in my absence, though yourself and Holmes are clearly the ranking officers here."

"There isn't anything else that can be done," agreed Lieutenant Prescott. "And believe me, my dear fellow, Holmes and I are not disturbed over seeing the command in the hands of officers whom we just happen to rank."

Hal, therefore, ordered his own sergeant and six men to remain on the prize, while the rest of the military party stepped over on to the "Restless." The two craft thereupon parted.

"Sergeant," ordered Overton, "you will see that this helmsman steers a straight course for Agua Dulce. Don't stand any nonsense from him. See that the start is made at once."

Just then Lieutenant Hal recalled the fact that he had left belt and revolver on a seat in the cabin. He went there, promptly, picked up the belt and buckled it on.

"Are you ready to talk business with me, now?" demanded the purple-faced one, in a low voice.

"I don't believe I care to have anything more to do with you," Hal retorted stiffly.

"Oh, go ahead and ruin me, then," snarled the stranger.

Hal, ascending to the deck, spoke to a soldier standing there.

"Rainsford, see that the man in the cabin does not come up on deck," Hal directed. "Keep your eye on him as the most important prisoner on this prize craft."

The purple-faced man stared after Hal Overton's retreating form.

"So you wouldn't come to terms, eh?" demanded the fellow, under his breath. "You'd rather ruin me. Two or three years in prison will ruin me, just at present, for my affairs will go to smash if I have to drop behind bars for a while. And if the government of Mexico finds that I have been helping the *insurrectos* it will mean total loss to me, perhaps, where my properties are situated in other parts of Mexico. And you, young whippersnapper in shoulder straps, you talked to me of your honor. Well, I'll pitchfork that honor of yours!"

The purple-faced man laughed harshly. He was in a deadly frame of mind.

Presently two soldiers came down, halting in the cabin doorway.

"We are ready, sir," spoke one of them.

"Ready for what?" jeered the stranger. "Have you come to shoot me?"

"We're nearing the dock at Agua Dulce, sir, and the lieutenant sent us to get you and make sure that you don't try to escape."

"I'll be bound that you won't give me any chance to get away," jeered the fellow.

"No, sir," answered the soldier gravely.

The Mexican helmsman proved that he was no mean boat-handler. He ran in alongside the dock, making nearly as fine a landing as Skipper Tom Halstead himself could have done. Lieutenant Hal waited only long enough for Corporal Shimple to send over two men from the tug in a row-boat to stand guard over the motor boat prize. Then, with his own boat squad, and leaving behind only the dead and the wounded Mexican, the Army boy marched his prisoners by a route that led around the village instead of through it.

Captain Foster had lain down, fully dressed, prepared to be called at any moment. He now came forth from his tent. He heard Lieutenant Hal's brief report with few interruptions.

"Your name, sir?" demanded Foster, turning to the purple-faced one.

"James D. Ruggles," came the surly answer.

"I hope you are giving your correct name."

"That's
the Money!"

"Why shouldn't I? If I gave you a wrong name there are plenty of people hereabouts who could soon set you straight."

"Your business, Mr. Ruggles?"

"Owner of mines in Mexico."

"Any in the *insurrecto* district?" pursued Captain Foster.

"Yes. That's why——"

Ruggles checked himself suddenly.

"You are not required to confess or incriminate yourself, unless you want to," Captain Foster advised the prisoner. "However, I imagine that the cargo of the boat and your actions to-night will furnish all the evidence against you that are needed. Mr. Ruggles, I shall have to hold you and your Mexican companions until I am advised what to do with you. There is no charge against your daughter. She may go to the hotel in Agua Dulce, if you wish. I will see to it that she is properly escorted."

"If you will be so good, Captain," answered Ruggles huskily. "But where shall I sleep to-night?"

"On a cot in the guard-tent, sir. I am sorry, but that is the best that we can do."

Meta Ruggles began to weep softly over her father's trouble and disgrace. Sergeant Raney, therefore, escorted her from camp as soon as he could persuade her to start for the village. Raney was also directed to send an undertaker for the body of the dead Mexican, and a local physician to look after the wounded one.

"You are going to sit here for a while, Captain?" inquired Ruggles.

"I think I shall."

"Then may I sit with you a few minutes before I am marched off to the guard-tent?"

"Certainly."

Hal had stepped into the tent shared in common by the officers. Ruggles, who had bitten the end from a cigar and had lighted the weed, now leaned over to whisper to Captain Foster:

"Has the young man had chance to give you a word or two of explanation yet?"

"What young man?" demanded Captain Foster, turning to look at Ruggles.

"Why, the officer who marched us over here."

"Lieutenant Overton?"

"Certainly. Has he told you anything? I mean about how this whole business is to be fixed so as to keep me out of it altogether?"

"What on earth are you talking about?" demanded Captain Foster, who was now wondering whether his ears had played him a trick.

"Why, it's all settled," murmured Ruggles.

"I turned the money over to your chap, Overton, and he told me it would be all fixed. I'm not to be held or prosecuted in this matter. The trouble is all to fall on the Mexicans."

"I wish I knew what you were talking about," cried Captain Foster.

"Why, it's plain enough, Captain. I paid the money over to your lieutenant, and he and you were to fix it so I could slide out of the matter and keep my name out, too. I paid Overton the five thousand dollars, which he said would be enough for you both and that it would be all right."

"Mr. Overton!" called Captain Foster gasping.

But Hal did not have to be summoned. He had heard Ruggles's last statement from the doorway of the officers' tent.

"Here I am, sir," cried Lieutenant Hal, coming forward, "and I overheard that lying hound! What this fellow, Ruggles, is telling you, Captain, is wholly false."

"I know it, Overton, I know it," cried Captain Foster, who had sprung to his feet.

"Am I to be flimflammed, after paying the money in good faith?" demanded Ruggles. "See here, Captain, I drew twenty thousand dollars, in twenty bills, at the bank this afternoon. That I can easily prove, of course. Nor can any one on earth prove that I have spent any of that money, for, as it happens, I had the cashier at the bank take the numbers of the thousand-dollar bills. In this envelope, sir, you will find fifteen of the bills left. The numbers of the missing bills can be proved, and the missing bills you will find in the possession of your lieutenant."

"It's a cowardly lie!" blazed thunderstruck Hal, leaping forward. But Captain Foster pushed him gently back.

"I haven't a doubt that it's a lie, Overton, my boy," replied Foster. "Yet don't get too excited, or try to use violence on your accuser. Remember that I am simply bound to hear any complaint that may be preferred against any officer in my command. Be cool, Overton, and be sure that no harm can come to you if you are innocent, as I am certain that you are. Here is your envelope, Mr. Ruggles. I have looked over the contents, which are, as you state, fifteen one-thousand-dollar bills."

"And the other bills you will find on this lieutenant. Though, wait a moment. He has just been in his tent. He may have hidden the money there."

"If it's true that you handed this lieutenant money, Mr. Ruggles, what did he do with it when he first received it?" asked Foster.

"I don't know, Captain, except that he went forward into the stateroom to look it over. He didn't have it in his hand when he came out of the stateroom."

"You——" quivered Hal.

"Easy, Overton, lad," admonished the captain. "Nothing is proved by calling another hard names. Take that chair, Mr. Overton, and wait until Sergeant Raney returns."

Pausing by the chair, before dropping into it, Hal faced his captain to say:

"I beg, sir, that you will order a search at once. I offer my person, my baggage—everything to be searched."

"I will have Sergeant Raney do it as soon as he returns," Captain Foster assured the angry young officer. "Raney is a wholly discreet fellow."

In time Sergeant Raney returned. He looked somewhat surprised when, after being taken into the officers' tent with his two superiors and Ruggles, Raney was ordered to begin a careful search of the lieutenant. Captain Foster stood where he could instantly have detected any effort that the Army boy might have made to throw any thing away.

Hal's first act was to unfasten his belt, and drop it, revolver and all, upon a chair. Then he straightened up, very white from the humiliation, yet absolutely sure, of course, that nothing damaging could be found upon him. Sergeant Raney went systematically through the young officer's pockets, searched for a money belt and failed to find one, explored his young officer's socks and shoes and even searched Hal's hatband.

88

"Now, the cartridge-box and revolver holster, Sergeant," insisted Captain Foster.

"And after that whatever baggage the young man may have," breathed Ruggles. "Also his bedding and——"

"Peace, sir!" commanded Captain Foster. "Wait until——"

Sergeant Raney, having opened Hal's revolver holster, now extracted a crumpled mass of folded bills!

"That's the money!" cried Ruggles, as Captain Foster unfolded the bills. "Read out the numbers, Captain, and we'll all take notes. I'll prove by the bank that this was my money earlier in the day!"

CHAPTER XXI

AMERICAN WOMEN IN PERIL!

SLOWLY Captain Foster read off the numbers, writing them down in a notebook that he carried. As the older officer glanced up he met the burning gaze of Lieutenant Hal Overton.

"Captain," cried the Army boy hoarsely, "I don't know by what juggling trickery this was done, but I never have handled that money, though it would seem that I must have been carrying it around in my holster."

"Bah!" sneered Ruggles.

Had it not been for Captain Foster's quick leap between the pair Hal would have knocked the purple-faced fellow down.

"Careful, Mr. Overton," warned the captain. "Violence will injure your case, not help it. Mr. Ruggles, I will hold this money as evidence, but I will give you a receipt for it."

"On that receipt will you enter the numbers of the bills?" demanded the purple-faced one craftily.

"Certainly," and Foster made the receipt out in that form, handing it to the promoter.

"Sergeant of the guard!" called Captain Foster.

Hal stiffened, his face turning ghastly. He felt that it would be better to die than to live a life of disgrace. The thought that he had been easily but cleverly tricked made his blood boil within him.

"Sergeant, conduct the prisoner Ruggles to the guard-tent, where the Mexicans are. Instruct the guard that they are to make absolutely sure that this prisoner doesn't escape."

"Doesn't your young man go to the guard-tent, too?" demanded Ruggles, as he stepped toward the sergeant.

"I will be responsible for the lieutenant," rejoined the captain coldly. "Thank you, Sergeant Raney. You may go. Of course you will be discreet."

When the two officers had the tent to themselves Foster turned his grave look on Hal Overton.

"My boy," said the captain, in a voice that shook, "I can't realize, even yet, that you have forfeited your honor as an officer."

"Nor have I, sir," returned Hal. "And I am even bold enough to hope that I can yet find some way of throwing the whole lie back in that fellow's throat with more proof than even he will care to swallow."

"I hope you can, Overton, with all my heart," responded the older soldier, resting a hand on his white-faced junior's shoulder.

"Do you believe me guilty, sir?" asked Hal, looking straight into his commander's eyes.

"Heavens knows I don't. To me, Overton, the whole thing seems absurd and incredible. But I am your commanding officer. A charge has been made that apparently destroys your honor. Some seeming proof against you has been found. There is only one course open to me. I must detain you in camp until I have communicated through the usual military channels."

"Am—am I under arrest?" asked Hal somewhat huskily.

"No, no, Overton!" exclaimed the older soldier quickly. "But you must give me your parole—not to go beyond camp limits at any time or for any purpose without my express permission."

"You have my parole, sir. It shall be rigidly observed."

"And now, Mr. Overton, I suggest that, as you have nothing else to do, you lie down and sleep through the night."

"*Sleep*, sir?" echoed Lieutenant Hal bitterly.

"Rest, then, at all events."

For two or three hours the Army boy lay and tossed. Toward morning, however, he secured some real sleep. When he opened his eyes it was to find Noll in the tent.

"I've heard the news, old bunkie," cried Terry, coming forward as soon as he saw his comrade's eyes open. "All rot! Forget it. It'll come out all right. When Prescott and Holmes heard the news they laughed aloud over the absurdity of it."

"I wish I was as sure of every one's faith in me," quivered the Army boy, returning his chums' hand-grip.

"Get up and dress. Captain Foster has had his meal, but the others are all waiting for you to hurry through to the table."

Three other young officers had crowded into the tent before Hal had finished dressing.

"The whole thing is absurd, Overton," declared Lieutenant Dick Prescott. "Holmesy and I have told Captain Foster so. We had you under our eyes in the Thirty-fourth during most of your more than three years of service. We know you too well to believe a word of any such fool charge against you."

"Even in the face of the money found in my holster?" asked Hal smiling wistfully.

"Huh!" retorted Lieutenant Greg Holmes. "It wouldn't shake our belief in you, old man, if the whole United States Treasury had been found hiding in your holster! Now, forget it all, as well as you can, Overton. Leave it to your friends, who will be cooler-headed, to find the way out from under this toy cloud. Why, even Foster knows it's all so absurd that he doesn't order you under arrest."

"Thank you all, fellows," replied Hal, his eyes gleaming as he shook hands with all three of his Army comrades and with the friend from the Navy. "I'll brace and fight every inch of the way. But," he could not help adding, wistfully, "I wish I could see how I am going to be able to clear myself so that not even a trace of a taint of suspicion can rest against any name."

The youngsters tried to make breakfast a merry meal, though they were not wholly successful. During the night, following the taking of the prize, Skipper Tom Halstead, it seemed, had been entertaining the four young officers left aboard the "Restless" with several exciting tales of his own wholly exciting life as a motor boat master. Most of these tales are already familiar to the readers of the "Motor Boat Club Series."

"What's Halstead's home port?" asked Hal, rather absently, for, naturally, his mind was rather full of his own troubles.

"Some little place near the mouth of the Kennebec River," Prescott answered.

"Then isn't he a long way from home?" asked Hal.

"Halstead often is a long way from home," nodded Lieutenant Holmes. "Not so very long ago Halstead commanded a yacht on the Pacific Ocean, and had some of his most rousing adventures at that time."

"It's young fellows like Halstead, Joe Dawson and that queer genius, Hank Butts, who are needed to build up the American merchant marine once more," Prescott continued.

Having been up all night most of the young officers were now glad to turn in for a few hours of sleep. Lieutenant Hal passed a wretched day of it.

Toward four o'clock in the afternoon an orderly brought in the afternoon mail from the village. With the mail came two telegrams, one for Captain Foster and the other for Lieutenant Prescott. That latter young officer tore open his telegram eagerly, and read:

"Received, en route, your telegram stating you were ordered to Holmesville. Belle and I at once changed our route and are here at Holmesville, Eagle Hotel. Mother with us. Find you not here, and no troops here, and that we will not be allowed to join your command. What shall we do?

"Laura Bentley."

"What a queer girl's freak that was," murmured Prescott, and called Ensign Dave Darrin over to read the despatch.

"I'm afraid I don't like that," muttered Dave, his brow darkening. "We'd better wire the girls begging them to get away from the border as soon as they know how."

"Who's that you're going to order away from the border, Mr. Darrin?" inquired Captain Foster, coming up and catching only a few words.

"No one that we can very well *order*, sir," replied Darrin. "I may as well tell the captain. You see, sir, Laura Bentley and Belle Meade are the two girl sweethearts that waited for us until we got settled in the service. They were on their way West to Fort Clowdry, for both girls wanted a military wedding, and there was nothing of that sort to be had in the home town. So Prescott wired them, aboard their train, that he was ordered to Holmesville, and that I was going along with him, and that we'd be back at Fort Clowdry at the earliest moment. But the girls took it into their head to change their route to

91

Holmesville. Maybe you can get away, Dick; in any case I'll hire an automobile and get up to Holmesville as quickly as I can."

"I am afraid there may be some difficulty about your getting into Holmesville, or the young ladies getting out," replied Captain Foster.

"What do you mean, sir?" demanded Prescott, noting how serious was the look on the captain's face.

"A few weeks ago, gentlemen, a mob burned a Mexican at the stake up at Holmesville. The Mexican was a worthless fellow, but of course an effort has been made to fasten the crime on the Texan residents of the town. As a matter of fact it is generally understood that the man lynched was burned by his own countryman as a result of some row among themselves. But the Mexicans on this border are in an ugly frame of mind, just now, as the most disorderly ones are all behind the revolution that's trying to get a start across the border. This telegram is from Washington, and informs me that the Mexicans have just turned loose at Holmesville. There are hundreds of them; they have been drinking and are armed. They greatly outnumber the Americans, and they are at present trying to get the upper hand in Holmesville."

"Riot and killing?" gasped Lieutenant Prescott, while Darrin's dark face went suddenly white.

"Yes," nodded Captain Foster.

"Then Prescott, we must get under way at once."

"You'll find it quite hopeless," remarked Captain Foster. "No man owning an automobile will take you into or near Holmesville until the rioting stops. The War Department advises me to have all in readiness to despatch troops by the river in case the governor of Texas calls for the help of United States troops."

"We ought to start an expedition up the river at once," groaned Lieutenant Dick Prescott, thinking of his and his friend's sweethearts in awful danger there.

"Unfortunately we can't start troops," replied the captain, "until the orders come. There are as yet no orders, and may not be."

"Then I must get under way alone," almost moaned Darrin. "You, too, Prescott, if you can get leave by 'phone from your commander."

"You can't get an auto," replied Captain Foster. "You'll have to walk, or go in saddle. Either course will take you nearly all of the night."

"But one of your boats, sir?" cried Prescott.

"You're an officer, Prescott, and you must realize that I can't legally release one of my boats from the duty here without an order or permission."

"And all the time Belle and Laura may be trying to hide from a blood-thirsty mob!" gasped Darrin in a frenzy.

"You stay here, Dick," broke in Greg Holmes. "I'll run to the nearest 'phone, get Captain Cortland at the other end of the wire, explain the situation to him and get leave to absent ourselves."

"But even at the best it will take hours to reach Holmesville," muttered Prescott, through blanched lips. "Oh, Dave, Dave, this is awful!"

"We'll get there, somehow—at least I will," muttered Ensign Darrin, in a quivering voice. "If you don't get leave within ten minutes, Dick, I'm going to start alone and try to run all the way to Holmesville. Captain Foster, you'll loan me a revolver and two boxes of cartridges, won't you?"

"Certainly," replied Foster, going into his tent and coming out with the articles named.

"I would like to make a suggestion, sir," broke in Lieutenant Hal.

"Go ahead, Mr. Overton," responded the captain.

"Why not send two men at once to the telegraph station? Order the telegraph office manager to remain open all night for military telegrams. If one comes, one of our men can start here at once on the run, leaving the other soldier to wait for a second despatch that may come in its wake."

"An excellent idea, Mr. Overton," and Captain Foster immediately sent two soldiers off on that errand.

"Sir, I request permission, if it can possibly be granted, to go with Darrin, Prescott and Holmes," broke in Lieutenant Noll.

"You may have that leave, certainly, Mr. Terry," replied Captain Foster.

"And I, also, Captain," broke in Hal eagerly, "since this affair involves the lives of the intended brides of two officers, and is most certainly a service affair."

"I fear you have forgotten something, Mr. Overton," replied Captain Foster gently. "You are now confined to camp, under charges."

Hal fell back, going suddenly white and staggering as though he had received a blow. In truth he had.

"I forgot," he assented wretchedly. "And, oh, this is hard, sir. I am wholly innocent of the charge, and yet of course you have no right to take my mere word. This, in the face of a desperate expedition that I want to join more than I ever wanted anything in my life as a soldier!"

CHAPTER XXII

SERGEANT KELLY'S FIT OF REMEMBERING

HOLMES was back with the speed of the wind. Even before he reached the camp he waved his cap, shouting:

"It's all right."

"And I'm going with you," Noll added.

"You, too, Overton?" demanded Lieutenant Greg Holmes.

"I can't," groaned Hal Overton.

"Oh, I beg your pardon, old chap," gasped Holmes, overcome with the thought of the humiliation he had needlessly caused this gallant young brother officer.

"I'm under charges, you know," remarked Hal, with a wan smile.

"Confound that Ruggles!" broke impetuously from Holmes's lips. "I'd almost like to burn him at a stake."

"Yes; it's tough," cried Prescott, "to be deprived of the help of one of the bravest, quickest-witted men in the United States Army!"

This heart-felt praise served as some balm to Hal's wounded, grief-stricken spirits. He would have given anything he possessed to join this long dash to save, if possible, two imperiled American girls.

"And there are other American women there to-night," added Hal brokenly.

None of the time was lost in talk, however, for the young officers who were to go were now busy looking to their weapons and ammunition, their canteens of water and other needed supplies.

It was unavoidable that the news should have leaked out among the soldiers now in camp.

The four young officers started soon, each giving Hal a silent, soul-felt grip of the hand before starting.

"Now, why the dickens ain't Lieutenant Overton going?" demanded Sergeant Kelly in wonder.

"Don't you know?" demanded a corporal. "Lieutenant Overton is in camp, under charges."

"What are ye talking about, man?" demanded Kelly incredulously.

"Oh, it's the truth," insisted the corporal.

"It's a frame-up, I am certain, but the prisoner, Ruggles, claimed that he gave the lieutenant five thousand dollars last night to fix it to let him, Ruggles, escape the consequences of smuggling arms over the border."

"What a silly lie!" sputtered Sergeant Kelly. "And did your captain believe a fool's fairy-tale like that?"

"He wouldn't have," replied the corporal, "only the lieutenant was searched, and the money was found hidden in his revolver holster."

"In the holster, say ye?" demanded Sergeant Kelly, with a flash of his eyes. The next words he uttered came in a shout:

"Binns, ye lop-sided shadow of a rookie!" he bellowed.

"Here, Sarge," answered a soldier, across a row of tents. "And what's got on your temper, Sarge?"

"Come here and ye'll be finding out!" growled Kelly, making a grab for the soldier. He caught that mystified fighting man, and, without a word, dragged him before Captain Foster.

"Salute the captain, ye deaf-mute!" ordered Kelly, letting go of the soldier and bringing his own hand up smartly to the brim of his cap.

"What's the meaning of these lightning tactics, Sergeant?" demanded Captain Foster.

"The meaning is, sir," ran on Kelly rapidly, "that I want this man to tell you something."

"What is it, my man?" demanded the captain.

"I don't know, sir," confessed Private Binns. "You'll have to ask Sergeant Kelly, sir."

"Binns," exploded Kelly, "you and me was standing at the stern on the captured motor boat for a spell, last night."

"We was—*were*," admitted Binns.

"Tell the captain what we saw when we looked down into the cabin, out of the darkness."

"Why we saw Ruggles handling Lieutenant Overton's revolver, in its holster," continued Private Binns.

"Now, what did the fellow Ruggles, do with the holster?" continued Sergeant Kelly severely.

"We saw him open the flap."

"And then?"

"Ruggles closed it again," stated Binns.

"Did we see him put anything in the holster?" cried Sergeant Kelly.

"Yes," admitted the soldier.

"What did it look like!"

"Paper—perhaps money," replied Binns slowly.

"D'ye think ye begin to see a light, Captain?" flashed Sergeant Kelly triumphantly. Then he turned to the soldier once more with:

"What did Ruggles do next?"

"He put the holster down and got up."

"How did he look?" pressed Kelly.

"Pleased, he looked. He grinned and muttered something quickly."

"Now, all that, Captain, sir, I'll swear to myself," continued the sergeant, turning in triumph to Captain Foster.

"Why didn't you tell me all this before?" demanded Captain Foster, while Hal stood by, all a-quiver, yet too full of emotion to speak.

"Because, sir, 'twas only a minute ago that I knew there'd be anything in our news. Binns and myself thought that Ruggles, when he picked up the lieutenant's revolver, had some notion of blowing out his brains. Had he taken the gun out of the holster we'd have jumped down into the cabin and taken it away from him. When he put the holster down, we concluded the fellow had only picked it up in a moment's curiosity. Then Binns and meself saw the lieutenant coming, and stepped away. I even thought, at the time, sir, that the paper was something that Ruggles had disturbed in the holster."

"Come with me to the guard-tent," ordered Captain Foster. "You, too, Mr. Overton!"

"Ah, ye scoundrel, I'm sorry I didn't throw ye overboard last night!" was Sergeant Kelly's warm greeting as his eyes fell upon Ruggles.

"Stand back, Sergeant. Don't use any violence on the prisoner," commanded Captain Foster.

Under the accusation that the sergeant poured forth Mr. Ruggles quickly wilted. Then he became sullen, refusing to admit any of the charges.

"I'll take the word of a good sergeant and an honest soldier," announced Captain Foster, turning and resting a hand on Hal's nearer shoulder. "Mr. Overton, Ruggles can prefer his charges at his leisure, if he wishes to, but as for me, until orders come from higher authority to the contrary, I inform you that you are no longer confined to camp. If there is time, Overton, you may run after the other young officers and go with them. I'll watch the river to-night myself."

"I'm afraid I can't overtake them now, sir," replied Hal, who, at least, was overjoyed at the appearance of this new and saving testimony. "I don't know just which road they've taken."

"Bugler!" shouted Captain Foster. As the field musician came running up he added: "Sound the recall. I think Prescott and the others will understand that.

95

Blow your hardest, Bugler. Give the call three times. That will bring them back, but every man among them, Overton, will think it worth while coming back briefly to add a fighting man like yourself to their number!"

Two or three minutes later the four young officers could be made out, coming back on the run.

At the same time one of the soldiers detailed at the telegraph office came up on the run from another direction.

CHAPTER XXIII

IN THE THICK OF THE RIOT

"WHAT is it, sir? *Troops* ordered out?"

"*Yes!*" cried Captain Foster, joyously, after a brief glance at the yellow sheet he had drawn from the envelope. "Listen. This order is from Washington. The War Department, acting on a request from the governor of Texas, has sent me the order direct to send twenty men and one or more officers up the river on the swiftest boat at my disposal. Mr. Overton, you will command. The other young officers will go with you. You, Mr. Prescott, will take your own ten men from the Thirty-fourth, and you, Mr. Overton, will take Sergeant Raney and nine men from this regiment. All the men are here at this moment. Rush the orders!"

As soon as the two sergeants had been called and had received the orders, Captain Foster continued his instructions.

"Gentlemen, you will use the troops only to save life and restore order in Holmesville. At the earliest possible moment you will turn control over to the local police again. You may have to fire into rioting crowds, but be careful about shooting recklessly or needlessly into groups. Remember, too, that there will doubtless be many estimable Mexicans at Holmesville who will not be rioters nor in any way in sympathy with them. The rioters, you will find, will be of the worst and most lawless class of Mexicans; they will be largely composed of refugees from Mexican justice—the very riff-raff of the population."

At the conclusion of the instruction the young officers broke for the officers' tent to get their swords. As this night might see rousing hand-to-hand work with rioters the swords might have their place.

The two sergeants heading the squads were now rushing the drawing of rations and ammunition. In a very few minutes the squads had fallen in.

"Sergeant Raney," called Lieutenant Hal, "move your squad to the dock in double time."

Prescott followed this with similar orders to Sergeant Kelly.

The two captured craft and the "Restless" lay at the dock. As the troops, their officers in the lead, marched out on the pier Skipper Tom Halstead sang out:

"Stand by the engine, Joe!"

With that the young motor boat captain leaped to the dock and ran to the stern hawser, while Hank Butts stood by the bow-hawser.

"Squad halt! Break ranks! Get aboard lively," ordered Sergeant Raney. Nor did Kelly let his own squad lose any time. The young officers followed in the wake of their men.

"Want to cast off?" called Skipper Halstead pleasantly.

"Without loss of a second," replied Lieutenant Hal.

Without waiting for other orders Hank let go the bow-line and carried it aboard with him. Tom Halstead went up over the stern.

"Slow speed ahead, Joe," Hank called down as he rested one hand on the wheel. The "Restless" began to move from her pier.

"Up river, or down?" called Skipper Tom, coming forward.

"Up!" voiced Hal. "And at racing speed, too!"

"Dutchman's gait, Joe," Hank called down unconcernedly, as soon as the "Restless" had well cleared the dock, having swung the craft around, heading up the river at a speed increased to twelve miles.

"Can't you crowd a lot more speed on?" demanded Hal Overton.

"Dog chasing that Dutchman, Joe," Hank sang down, and the "Restless" was soon doing eighteen miles an hour.

"You told me your best speed was twenty-six to twenty-eight, didn't you?" asked Hal, wheeling around as Skipper Tom Halstead joined them.

"Yes, sir."

"Can you hit up that speed without endangering the engine?"

"Yes," replied Tom, "but we'll burn a lot of gasoline doing that."

"Gasoline?" uttered Prescott contemptuously.

"How many pailfuls will a thousand dollars buy?"

"Is it as bad as that?" asked Skipper Tom quickly.

"American women's lives are at stake up at Holmesville!" returned Overton. "Riot going on there—Mexicans against Americans."

Hank Butts didn't wait for orders.

"Joe," he yelled, bending over the engine-room doorway, "sheriff and a bill-collector after that Dutchman!"

Joe Dawson didn't wait to be told more. He threw open everything to the widest notch, then snatched up a bulky oil can with an unusually long spout, and stood feeding oil to the bearings.

"The sweethearts of Mr. Prescott and Mr. Darrin are in great danger at Holmesville," Lieutenant Hal murmured in Skipper Tom's ear.

"Jumping Jupiter!" gasped Halstead, and went down into the engine-room in two bounds for a word with Joe.

Those standing on the deck could fairly feel the quiver with which the "Restless" leaped forward at her best speed.

"It's like riding on an express train!" glowed Lieutenant Greg Holmes.

"No express train was ever made that's fast enough for me to-night," muttered Lieutenant Dick Prescott between set teeth.

The running lights were out, for it was nearly dark when the "Restless" had left Agua Dulce. Only the movement of a switch was needed to turn them on.

"Ever been to Holmesville?" demanded Dave Darrin, turning almost fiercely on Tom Halstead when he showed his head on deck.

"No, sir."

"Wouldn't know the place by sight?"

"No, sir."

"Nor I, either—from the water front," groaned Darrin. "But surely you have some chart of the river?"

Tom Halstead was already out of sight again. When he came on deck he remarked:

"I've been looking at the chart. Now, I'll know Holmesville to a dot when we sight the place."

"Nice sort of a town some one took the trouble to name after me, isn't it?" grunted Lieutenant Holmes.

"Say! Look there!" gasped Lieutenant Noll, pointing ahead just as the craft rounded a bend of the river, and something was visible that the trees had shut out before.

A thrill of dismay went through all. Ahead the sky was angrily red at one point.

"The miscreants have fired the town!" roared Dick Prescott, in anguish. "Captain Halstead, is there no more speed to be wrung out of this boat?"

"We're going like the wind, now, Mr. Prescott," Halstead answered. "To try for any more speed would be to endanger either the engine or the propeller."

"Let this young skipper alone, Dick," whispered Holmes soothingly, in his chum's ear. "He knows his business, if ever a man did!"

As more miles were covered the red blur against the dark sky became larger and brighter. Prescott and Darrin watched it as though dazed. Once in a while their hands wandered to their weapons.

"We'll be there in ten minutes more," announced Halstead finally, after a glance at his watch.

"Thank Heaven!" devoutly muttered two young officers.

"Oh, I hope we're *in time!*" groaned Lieutenant Hal, turning to Noll Terry.

Three or four enlisted men were on deck. The others, after the cool indifference of their kind until the moment of action comes, were below in the cabin. But every soldier started to his feet as Raney's voice rang out:

"Ready, men, for a quick landing!"

"You'll go back out into the stream, won't you, Halstead?" Lieutenant Overton asked, as Hank directed the "Restless" in toward a dock.

"Joe Dawson will," answered Skipper Tom. "He and I have already drawn lots to see which one of us would stay on the boat."

"You're not going ashore into this hades of riot and arson, are you?"

"Where American women are in danger?" retorted Skipper Tom. "Nothing less than a file of soldiers could keep me back!"

A dozen irregular shots rang out just as Halstead and Hank leaped ashore to hold the lines.

"Tumble off there, men. Don't wait for any gang-plank!" roared Lieutenant Prescott.

Tom Halstead and Hank Butts did not attempt to throw the hawsers over posts, but tossed their lines back to the deck as soon as the last soldier was ashore. Joe

Dawson, taking his place at the wheel, and with one foot against the deck control of the engine, bawled out:

"Good luck to every one of you!"

Hal Overton had swiftly formed his squad in a single rank, ordering the soldiers to fix bayonets. Prescott formed his own squad as a second platoon. As Tom Halstead hastened up he carried a stout cudgel, while Hank Butts carried the hitching weight that had made him famous.

As the little relief column moved off the dock and in at the foot of the principal street of Holmesville, the light of burning buildings showed them a highway on which hundreds of maddened human brutes were moving.

Occasionally, from one of the houses still left untouched by flames, a shot was fired. So enraged and occupied were the rioters that they did not perceive the approach of uniformed men.

"Forward, on the double quick!" ordered Lieutenant Hal, snatching his sword from the scabbard. Just ahead the rioters had turned to pour a fusillade of fifty shots into a house from which a revolver shot had been fired.

There was no sense in halting and calling on these maddened rioters to disperse. Hal saw that quickly. Some in the mob saw the soldiers in time to raise a shout, but few of the other rioters heard it.

"Ready to charge! *Charge!*" shouted Lieutenant Hal Overton.

The front rank of soldiers hit the edge of the mob with cold steel. That rush and impact seemed to serve only to madden the rioters, and in an instant there was wild hand-to-hand combat.

CHAPTER XXIV

CONCLUSION

THEN a score of things happened all at once.

Added to the soldiers' bayonets the swords of four young officers thrust with an effect that opened a way up through the mob.

"*Los soldados!*" sounded a score of voices at once. On top of this came another cry in frantic Spanish: "*Al muerto!*" (to the death!)

One short, broad-shouldered fellow rushed at Lieutenant Hal from the flank, knife uplifted. Hank dropped his hitching weight on the fellow's toes, and the knife-thrust fell short by some three feet. Tom Halstead's cudgel floored a rascal who aimed a revolver at Hank.

The first squad went through the crowd fast, though leaving a red trail of minor sword and bayonet wounds. The second squad had a harder fight, as the enraged mob, after spreading a bit, closed in. There was still plenty of fight in the rioters, who now realized how small a military force had assailed them. Dave Darrin was using the butt of the borrowed revolver in clubbing every strange head that got within reach of his arm.

"Halt! About face and go back into 'em!" ordered Lieutenant Hal. The mob, feeling itself hemmed in between two parallel lines of bayonets, gave sufficiently to let the military party reunite.

"Where's the Eagle Hotel?" Hal shouted hoarsely, as a Texan, rifle in hand, showed himself at an open window.

"Two blocks up. You can't mistake it!" came back the roaring answer.

As the two ranks of soldiers tried to go on at the double quick, two or three hundred of the mob tried to follow at their heels.

"Second squad halt! About face!" yelled Lieutenant Prescott. "Load! Aim!" Then he turned to his chum.

"Fire if you have to, Holmesy. I've got to leave you and run forward!"

Lieutenant Greg Holmes nodded his understanding. Then he stood there, grim-faced and watchful, mindful, also, of his orders not to fire on rioters unless it became absolutely necessary.

But the sight of ten Army rifles staring them in the face caused the mob to halt for a moment or two, whereupon Holmes faced his men about, continuing the march. Twice more he found it necessary to halt and menace the enraged followers.

Ahead was another mob not much smaller. These men were in front of the Eagle Hotel as the first squad ran up.

"Charge!" yelled Lieutenant Hal. "Charge!" echoed Greg Holmes. There was another sharp, ugly clash. Bayonets prodded, swords thrust, Tom Halstead wielded his club and Hank was busy with his weight.

Dave, Dick and Noll, as soon as they could reach the hotel, dashed away from the troops toward the front entrance of the hotel, which stood open, battered down as it had been by the mob.

As these three rescuers darted into the lobby, a woman's scream sounded from a room not far away. Into this dashed the three young officers. Just before they vanished Tom Halstead and Hank Butts rushed in, catching sight of their friends.

In the billiard room of the hotel stood Mrs. Bentley, leaning against a wall and looking ready to faint. Laura Bentley, far more beautiful than when we saw her last, had caught up a chair, with which she was threatening a dark-haired young Mexican who sought to reach her. Belle Meade, her dark beauty unmarred by the look of anger in her face, had snatched up a cue, with which she was menacing another young Mexican dandy. Four or five other Mexicans stood in the room, interested spectators.

"A reminder for you, my friend!" muttered Dick Prescott hoarsely, as he ran his sword-point into the thigh of the man before Laura.

"May this give your mind ease!" gritted Ensign Darrin, bringing down the butt of the revolver on the head of the Mexican facing Belle.

Then the other Mexicans in the room attempted to take a hand, but they were soon put to flight. One of them limped, or rather hopped—for he had encountered Hank Butts. Tom and Hank helped the injured out in a hurry.

Mrs. Bentley revived at sight of the uniforms, and still more at sight of the well-known faces of two of the officers. As for Laura, she threw her arms about Dick Prescott's neck, embracing him ecstatically, too overjoyed at first to speak. Not so with Belle Meade. She, too, gave her intended husband an enthusiastic embrace, but she murmured in his ear:

"Sorry we couldn't give a better account of ourselves, Dave. But the scoundrels came in here in a drove. They've killed at least two men who tried to defend us."

"If they try to start anything more, Belle, girl, they'll all get killed."

Lieutenant Dick Prescott, a mist swimming before his eyes, could only murmur:

"Laura, you need have no further fears. There are squads from two regiments of regulars on the spot."

Presently Dick and Dave were left behind at the hotel with five soldiers of the Thirty-fourth. Lieutenant Hal led the remainder of the troops through the streets. The comparatively few Texans of the village, who had been greatly outnumbered, and driven to fighting behind cover, now appeared in the wake of the troops. Wherever bands of rioters were found they were herded and driven out of the town. It required all the firmness and tact of Lieutenant Hal to keep the justly enraged Texans from piling up a big slaughter.

Before the arrival of troops some twenty Mexican rioters had been killed, and many more wounded. Six of the Texans of the village had also been killed, including the two—the hotel proprietor and one other—who had gone to the defense of Mrs. Bentley and the girls. A score of rioters who had met Hank Butts were limping now.

Thirty houses of the village, some of them belonging to Mexicans, had been fired. As they were not attached to other buildings these fires were allowed to burn out.

At daylight a company of Texas militia marched into town, having arrived from a distant point.

The rioters belonged to a peculiar class from the sister republic. Many were criminals, wanted in their own country, who had found safety across our border. Many more had been of the class who would have been camp followers of the insurgent army, had that especial revolution gained the dignity of being backed by a rebel army.

For three weeks more the border patrol was continued. Then, as the revolutionists over in Mexico had been soundly thrashed by the responsible federal government of Mexico, the border patrol by our own American troops was no longer needed.

As early as possible Laura Bentley, Belle Meade and Laura's mother were escorted to the railway, and sent forward to Fort Clowdry, there to wait as Mrs. Cortland's guests until Prescott could return from Texas. Dave Darrin, of course, went along with the ladies.

Ruggles, who had once been worth some three million dollars, mostly invested in Mexico, never dared press his absurd charge against Lieutenant Hal Overton. As a result of the revolution, and his known part in it, Ruggles had much of his Mexican property confiscated under the laws of that country. The rest of his estate dwindled sadly for want of his care, for Ruggles, owing to his orders to fire on United States troops, was sent to a federal prison for ten years.

Guarez, Boggs and a few others were given prison sentences of two or three years each.

Of the two boats captured, Boggs's tug was released on payment of a fine. Ruggles's motor boat, however, was condemned and sold at auction. Ruggles's daughter, Meta, his sole near relative, is now living on the remnant saved out of her father's fortune. She is a good girl, and is waiting to aid her parent to begin life over again when he is freed.

Tom Halstead and his boatmates, as soon as released from the government contract, departed in search of further adventures. That they found them is known to readers of the volumes in the "Motor Boat Club Series."

A month after the affair at Holmesville there was as picturesque a double service wedding as it was possible to have at Fort Clowdry.

The Thirty-fourth's band furnished the music. The post chapel was the scene of the solemn affair. All the parents of the contracting parties came on from Gridley.

The chapel was ablaze with all the pomp and glory of the dress uniforms of the Army and the Navy, for a few of Dave's brother officers contrived to be present.

Greg Holmes was, of course, Prescott's best man; Ensign Dan Dalzell performed that service for Ensign Dave Darrin.

Nor were Lieutenants Hal and Noll absent, for they secured leave to attend. The ushers at the wedding were four young naval officers, with Hal, Noll, Algy Ferrers and another young lieutenant representing the Army.

Behind the double bridal party, as the post chaplain and an assistant began the solemn, beautiful service of the church, stood the ushers, a double wall of steel, as it struck some of the onlookers—a wall of Army and Navy steel guaranteeing the future of the two young couples and pledging them happiness.

Lieutenants Hal Overton and Noll Terry were now firmly established in their new careers as line officers of the United States Army. At the next session of Congress the Senate ratified their nominations as a matter of course, and the two young officers soon after received their commissions as second lieutenants from the President.

Though of course it was far beyond the reach of their present vision, a deep shadow was hanging over the world—the shadow of a great war to come, the greatest and most savage war in the history of the world. In that coming war with the German Empire, each of these splendid young officers was destined to play a big part, a part that was certain to bring honors to each, as well as the appreciation of a grateful country.

The story of their participation and of their thrilling experiences in this great world war, will be told in a following volume, entitled "Uncle Sam's Boys With Pershing's Troops at the Front; Or Dick Prescott at Grips With the Boche."

The End.

CPSIA information can be obtained at www.ICGtesting.com
Printed in the USA
LVOW11s1232010414

379825LV00050B/1996/P